a New Home

The Pleiadian Perspective on Ascension

BOOK ONE

BY **Suzanne Lie**

http://www.multidimensions.com

http://www.suzanneliephd.com

CA Times Publishing, Los Angeles

Table of Contents

Final Thoughts

A Glimpse of Book Two of Pleiadian
Perspectives on Ascension
Additional Information about the Author

How it All Began

It's April eleventh 2012, and the California sun was still below the horizon. After a long complex dream of being in someone else's house and realizing it was time for me to leave and go to my own house, I woke up at 5:55 with the words, *Transmissions from Home!*

I got up and went into my office to receive this transmission. I am ready for your transmission now. Would you please send me your message? Then I heard the words again, "Transmissions from Home."

In my mind's eye I saw a man sitting at a desk looking like a newscaster. He was blond and had on a uniform, which I thought looked like the Uniform of a member of the Galactic Federation.

His uniform was white and gold with an insignia over his heart. There were also golden adornments on his shoulders, and his collar was straight up, like a military uniform.

In fact, it was a dress military uniform, but not from our military.

After hearing twice that he had "Transmissions from Home," I turned on my computer, put my hands over the keyboard and prepared my consciousness for his message by saying,

"I am ready for your transmission."

I was surprised when the first message came from a female named Mytria.

A New Home

Suzanne Lie

Pleiadian Perspective on Ascension
BOOK ONE

PART ONE

A New Home

Finding Freedom

Beloved Ones,

I am Mytria from the Violet Temple of Transmutation on Alcyone, Pleiades. I AM a higher expression of the one who is writing. I am here to remind all of you that you ALL have many higher expressions of your Multidimensional SELF in the fifth dimension and beyond.

I encourage you all to allow your higher expressions to communicate with you in whatever fashion best suits the personality of your present incarnation. Some of you will best communicate with words. Others will be guided by another creative expression such as music, dance, art, and athletics, or working with nature, prayer and a myriad of other expressions of your innate creative force.

You will know when you are connected to your higher expression by the shift in your consciousness and the release of the constant demands of your ego. We, your expressions of SELF in higher frequencies of reality, are reaching out to you to assist you during your return to your true Multidimensional SELF.

We remind you to trust that your imagination, your love-filled thoughts and emotions, sudden creative ideas, and fulfilling dreams are direct messages from your SELF. Since you all have myriad higher expressions of SELF, you may feel communications from many of us. Do not be confused by these many voices, as we are all connected in the ONE to draw you into your greater experience of SELF.

The Pleiadians and the Arcturians have been aligned in like-minded service for millions of your years. We also serve on Star Ships together. Therefore, as you look into your vast history of higher dimensional realities, if you find the Arcturians, you will likely find the Pleiadians, as well. The Arcturians remind you of the great power of your unconditional love and multidimensional light, whereas we Pleiadians may remind you of your joy of living, dancing, singing, being with friends and experiencing inter-personal love relationships.

The Arcturians represent your tenacity to "stay the Path of Ascension," and the Pleiadians remind you to dance, sing, create and love throughout your entire process of ascension. The Arcturians remind you of your deepest spiritual love, whereas we remind you to love life within every moment. Of course, both of our civilizations contain all the qualities that we have mentioned, but even Galactics have specialties.

Furthermore, Arcturian realities resonate to the higher-fifth dimension and beyond where all thoughts, emotions and desires are instantly fulfilled. Since our Pleiadian world has ascended much more recently than Arcturus, we have taken on the honor of assisting you in creating your fifth dimensional, threshold society of New Earth.

Just as the Arcturians, Pleiadians, Sirians and members of the Ashtar Command are assisting you from the Galactic realms; the Lemurians are assisting from the core of Gaia, as well as from the core of your ancient memories. In other words, we have you covered from "above" and "below."

Of course, above and below are metaphorical terms, as we are all resonating to the fifth dimension and beyond. However, some of you will feel the need to align yourselves with the Lemurians, others with the Arcturians and others with the Pleiadians.

When you fully regain your multidimensional consciousness, you will no longer need to choose between your myriad expressions of SELF, as you will be able to easily align yourself with ALL of us. Since we are aligned with each other, when you connect with any of us, you bond with all of us. Furthermore, as you experience the first "recognition of your multidimensional nature, you will merge with as many higher dimensional expressions of your SELF as your consciousness can accept within that frequency of consciousness.

You see, dear ascending ones, there is NO end of you. Also, there is NO beginning of you. You are timeless energy signatures of multidimensional light and unconditional love that adheres to whichever versions of reality attracts you within the NOW of the ONE. Some realities are a short visit, but others are a commitment that encompasses many eons of experience. Some realities have "time," in which you age and go through different cycles of life. On the other hand, some worlds are timeless, and you can "live" there until you decide to detach your consciousness from that matrix.

Polarities are only known in the worlds ruled by time, as time creates separation, limitations and the extremes of polarity. However, realities that resonate to the mid-fifth dimension and beyond function in no time. Hence, there is no aging, separation, limitation or extremes.

While time-worlds are useful for learning many lessons quickly, it is easy to forget your SELF and become trapped in that reality. Conversely, life in the mid-fifth dimension and beyond allows you to maintain the same form or signature frequency until you feel complete with that experience and decide to move on to your next adventure.

After many higher dimensional realities, you may want to have the challenge of a polarized world. On the other hand, after a long run in the polarized spectrum of the lower frequency adventures, you may wish to rest, rejuvenate, love, and spiritually expand in the higher worlds.

What we are saying is that there are no GOOD worlds or BAD worlds. These judgments are confined to the time-based worlds of polarity. There are only choices of experience. Fortunately, since you are a multidimensional being, you can make many choices all within the same "time." However, you will not be able to recognize this fact from a time-bound world.

Time-bound worlds force you to grow, whereas timeless worlds allow you to expand. Now, our dear returning ones, you are feeling complete with growing for a while and are ready to return to the more expansive versions of your SELF. When you have done so, the constant self-judgment, fear and struggle will be no more. Once you have chosen to return to your higher expressions of SELF, you will regain a freedom that was lost with your first physical incarnation.

However, in order to fully "return to SELF," you must completely and unconditionally love, forgive and accept the YOU that you have chosen to express in your present incarnation. Hence, please do not judge yourself that you have done something wrong or another thing right.

These judgmental concepts only arise from the limitations of third dimensional thinking and are riddled with conditional love. Third dimensional thinking and love based on conditions bind you to the third dimension. In order to return to the timeless expressions of your SELF, you need to master your thoughts and emotions.

Many of our returning ones are asking, "What can I do to ascend?" To this question we respond, "Our dear returning ones, to break through the final illusions of your physical containment, ***think beyond time*** and ***love without condition***. Once you can do that for yourself, you are FREE to assist others to do the same.

A New Home

Returning to Our Multidimensional SELF

Mytria from Alcyone

I AM MYTRIA, KEEPER OF THE VIOLET FLAME ON ALCYONE, PLEIADES.

I AM MYTRE, COMMANDER IN THE ASHTAR COMMAND.

We are Divine Complements and are one of the higher expressions of this writer. We come to you as ONE being to speak with you about the joining of many Divine Complements as our beloved Earth comes into Her fifth dimensional expression. As you all know, Gaia (including all Her inhabitants) is expanding Her frequency back into the fifth dimension and beyond. Hence you, the ascending ones of Earth, will be re-connecting with the completeness of your male and female expressions by reuniting with your Divine Complements.

When you first entered the third dimension, Earth was a polarized reality. Therefore, it was necessary for your innate androgynous expression to choose a body of gender. Then, as you continued your many incarnations on physical Earth, you expressed yourself as either a man or a woman. Your Divine Complement has gone through the same process. Hence, both of you have had myriad incarnations of both male and female earth vessels. However, as you ascend into the fifth dimension, your polarity of form will no longer be necessary. Therefore, if you choose, you can unite with the completeness of your androgynous, Multidimensional SELF.

In order for you to fully understand what we are about to say, we ask that you read our story with your multidimensional thinking. We introduced our SELF as our two extremes of feminine and masculine expression. It is true that you have perceived higher dimensional beings in male or female forms as some of us, especially Pleiadians, still enjoy holding a masculine or feminine form. However, we are always intimately connected with our Divine Complement. Since time and space do not exist in the fifth dimension in the same manner as in the physical world, one of us can be on our Homeworld and the other in a Starship traveling the Universe without feeling any sense of separation.

We can do so because we returned to our true, multidimensional nature when we ascended back into the fifth dimension. Thus, we can experience two or more realities within the same moment of the NOW. In other words, we experience our life as ONE being who is experiencing two (in fact many more than two) realities at once. It is because of this last sentence that we asked you to think multidimensionally. In fact, we have come to you at this time to assist you in thinking multidimensionally so that you can more easily understand and fully participate in your ever-ascending reality.

We will be telling you some of our experiences of ascension when we Pleiadians returned to our fifth dimensional expression. Unlike our dear friends the Arcturians, we are a civilization that very much enjoys the expression of a form. The Arcturians ascended long before us, but we remained in continual contact, as our civilizations have been inter-twined for longer than your time could count. In fact, many of our ascending ones on Earth have higher expressions, and ongoing lives/experiences, in both the Pleiadian and Arcturian worlds.

The concepts of *life* and *expression* have the same meaning to a multidimensional being, as we do not need to "be born" and "die." Instead, we choose to engage in a certain form/reality until we feel complete with that experience. Then we merely exit that reality, but we remember every experience of every reality in which we have participated. We know that this extent of memory seems impossible to your third dimensional thinking, but we assure you that is consistent with all life forms of the fifth dimension and beyond.

Those of you who are awakening to your higher expressions, which are only *higher* to the perception of your earth vessel, understand what we are saying. For those who have not yet had that experience, what we are saying likely seems impossible. However, we want to encourage you to release the concept of *impossible* from your thinking patterns, as you are about to enter into a new life in which impossible is probable. For example, many of you will be meeting a grounded one, or a higher dimensional one, whom you believe to be your Divine Complement or Twin Flame.

In some cases, you are realizing that your Divine Complement is one whom you have been close to for many years. In other cases, you may have a chance meeting with someone that you know within your heart is your Complement. Sometimes you are able to enter into an intimate and lasting relationship with that person, but sometimes that person must leave your life for a reason that is difficult for you to accept. If the second example is the case, it is often because it is important that both of continue your *Reason for Incarnation* alone.

In this case, you are both creating a pyramid of ascension by maintaining your physical connection via your consciousness while you both focus on your already united SELF in the fifth dimension. If this is the situation, it is because you both made that choice before you took your present form. From your timeless state in the fifth dimension, a mere lifetime of separation was insignificant in comparison to the contribution that you would give to Gaia by anchoring your joint consciousness with each other and with your fifth dimensional unified expressions.

In fact, most of the sacrifices that our ascending ones have had to make were chosen before birth to either awaken you to your SELF and/or to assist with Planetary Ascension. As you continue to return to your timeless, multidimensional thinking, the hardships of your life so far will be erased from your memory. Only that which you have learned from these hardships is of importance to your ascension process. Hence, as a benefit of participating in Gaia's ascension, you will find that fear-based experiences will begin to disappear from your memory.

These fear-based experiences will become similar to a bad tasting medicine you had to take. You did not enjoy the medicine, but you are happy that it made you well. In the same manner, your past hardships where chosen by your Multidimensional SELF to assure that unfinished business that had lowered your consciousness for myriad lifetimes, be resolved and released. Once you have become the Victor of many of your past experiences of victimization, you will understand what we are saying.

To become trapped in the past is to become trapped in time. And, to become trapped in time is to become trapped in the third/fourth dimension. Therefore, you have chosen to write some unpleasant experiences into your Birth Contract to force yourself to forget the pain and suffering and move on to create a new, better life. You see, dear ascending ones, what you are doing within your personal release of *time* and all its problems, is vital to assist Gaia to free Her from Her myriad fear-based experiences of "raising" humanity.

Of all Her children, humanity was the most challenging. Her plants and animals never forgot that they were a component of Her form. However, humanity was so intent on gaining *power-over others* that they even chose to conquer the very Earth that allowed them to experience incarnation. We wish to tell you that Gaia is so happy that so many of Her humans have found their *power-within* and no longer need to experience *power-over others*. In fact, as the darkness/fear is being released by humanity, Gaia's frequency is rising beyond the resonance of a fear-based realty.

We, along with Gaia, remind you again that the most important contribution you can give to Planetary Ascension is to REFUSE to participate in any form of fear. This includes all forms of anger and sorrow. This request is one that we could not ask of our ascending ones until your moment of the NOW of ascension. With the return of cosmic energy patterns that only enter Earth once every 26,000 years, our ascending ones MUST release that which is over, in order to embrace that which is commencing.

We, the members of your Galactic Family, are HERE to assist your NOW!

Blessings from,

Mytria/Mytre of the Pleiades

Two Realities at Once

GREETINGS FROM MYTRIA, MYTRE AND THE ARCTURIANS:

We would like to take you on a multidimensional journey. Please, just relax and enjoy the ride while we guide you in an exercise to assist you to remember your true, multidimensional nature…

Begin by seeing yourself aboard our Starship, Athena. There are many Pleiadians and Arcturians on this Ship working as ONE to assist humanity and Gaia with the great transition. Imagine yourself in a Corridor of the Ship. Now walk over to the wall and touch it to connect with the life force of the Ship. You can feel that the Ship is happy to assist and guide you on your journey. Yes, the Ship itself will guide you, for it is a living being.

As you connect with the Ship, many memories flash into your awareness. These memories are multidimensional in that they are of experiences you have had as your fifth dimensional SELF. Close you eyes so that you can more easily allow these memories to enter into your physical brain.

Imagine these memories as pictures and feelings as you:

• Look down to your feet and see what you have

on them…

• Look at your legs. What do they look like and what is covering them…

• Look at what you are wearing…

• Look at your hands and your arms…

Now that you have grounded your Essence in this reality:

• See yourself embracing old comrades from your many visits to this ship…

• Feel how their greeting warms your heart…

• Notice how they encircle you and welcome you back from your "away mission"…

• Hear their voices and look into their eyes…

• Reach out to touch them and feel their touch on you…

Most of these old friends have extended their consciousness into one of their earth-bound expressions and are eager for that component of their beingness to return into their Multidimensional SELF. These friends know that your Mission on Earth is not yet complete and that this meeting is only a visit.

Between visits you may spend much of your leisure time imagining a reality that seems so distant from your earth life, yet it will not totally leave your memory. This memory is a blessing, and feels like letters from home when you are far away. In fact, your Earth life is quite similar to a "tour of duty." However, this tour of duty will last for the duration of your Mission.

When you first began to awaken, you could only long for that which was missing. Gradually, that longing forced you to go deep within to find the answers that were invisible to your physical world. Now you have found many answers and are sharing them with others. Fortunately, there are more and more *others* with whom you can be open. In fact, openly being your SELF is an important part of your Mission. However, you do not wish to think about Earth right now, for you are temporarily home on your Starship.

When the time-bound thought of "temporarily" enters your mind, your vision of being on the Ship fades. Instantly, you close your eyes to regain your connection with your higher expressions of reality. You focus intently on the feeling of the Ship's wall. It feels almost like skin, not in texture, but because it feels alive. The memory of "things" being without life in your 3D world floods into your awareness and the hall begins to fade again. You focus intently on the feeling of the living wall and slowly maintain your connection to this higher dimensional reality.

While holding that image firmly in your awareness, you ponder how your physical form will ever contain this multidimensional awareness. Fortunately, you refuse to participate in doubt. You focus on the FACT that different frequencies of reality feel different. Your physical world has stark contrasts. "Things" have edges and hard boundaries and walls are hard and without life.

However, as you take a moment to partially

open your eyes, you can see a faint emanation from every "thing" that you once thought of as non-living. In fact, as you look across the room, you see a vague emanation from the wall. Your eyes drift to a plant, a person or an animal to see how their emanation is much stronger.

As you look at the wall of your physical room, you see the overlay of the wall in the Starship, and you gradually return your awareness to the Starship. However, instead of trying to ignore your physical world while you travel inter-dimensionally, you hold BOTH worlds in your ever-expanding multidimensional consciousness.

- First, with your eyes partially open, you look around your area to see the many auras and/or electrical emanations. You *SAVE* that image to your mind, and close your eyes, maintaining the image.

- Now, see the Starship again. You are alone in the corridor with your hand on the wall, and you hold that image as well. Now, close your physical eyes to block out your physical world and open your Third-eye to perceive your fifth dimensional world…

- Next, maintaining the image of your hand on the Starship's wall, open your eyes to your 3D world—BUT keep your awareness of the Starship active in your consciousness by keeping your Third Eye open…

• Finally, with your physical eyes open to your physical world, maintain an opened Third Eye in your fifth dimensional world…

This exercise is how we, the Pleiadians, began our ascension into the fifth dimension. We had Starship travel before our ascension, but we also had many wars and conflicts. We began to tire of conflicts and battle. We are by nature a gentle people and would much prefer to dance, sing, create art, enjoy our friends and engage in amorous activities. The harshness of competition, battle and conflict hurt our Souls and lowered our frequency.

Then we found our home in the Pleiades open cluster. The Pleiades, also known as the "Seven Sisters," is a cluster of young stars. Barely 50 million years ago, the Pleiades cluster was formed from a collapsing cloud of interstellar gas. The biggest and brightest members of this cluster are blue-white and even the faintest stars are about 40 times more luminous than your Sun. The star Alcyone A is about 100 times brighter than your Sun.

Finding our new home was the first real safety we had experienced since we had left our Homeworld of Lyra. As soon as we arrived here, we knew that we could develop a life that was akin to the callings of our Soul. Therefore, our dear ascending ones, we know how extremely difficult it has been for you to begin and go through your ascension process while you are living in a war zone. In fact, we literally understand your feelings, for many of us have taken an Earthly incarnation to assist the ascension from the body of Gaia.

We Pleiadians have enjoyed many incarnations/visits on Earth. We say *incarnations/visits* for we only experienced our lives there as incarnations before we ascended into the higher frequencies. Now we perceive our earthly forms as visits, log-ins, or choices to experience being on third dimensional Earth. Also, many of us have volunteered to share our emanation with our grounded expression, to over-light their choice to incarnate on ascending Gaia.

Now that we resonate to multidimensional consciousness, we can constantly experience our life in our home world, on our Starship and in a physical form within the same NOW of the ONE. Our grounded expressions are often unaware of the other realities that are running parallel to their physical self.

It is the return of your multidimensional perceptions that marks your conscious return Home to your higher expressions of SELF. Therefore, we encourage our beloved human brothers and sisters to remember that they are NOT and have NEVER been trapped on Earth. Only a very small segment of your Multidimensional SELF is living the experience of your physical earth vessel.

That earth vessel has been closed to all multidimensional input until very recently in your *time*. As you return to your SELF, you will find great comfort in returning to your Homeworld, your Starship and your higher dimensional Temples. These visits will gradually become similar to *going home* after a long day of work. When you go to work, you do not expect that your house will leave while you are away. In the same manner, your higher expression of SELF does not disappear because you are placing your primary attention on your physical reality.

Learning to simultaneously contain more than one experience of reality in your consciousness is the basis of returning to your Multidimensional SELF. At first, you will only be able to have one *primary* reality at a *time*, but as you release your attachment to time, you will find that you can consciously live more than one reality as an on-going experience. You will begin by living two realities at once and have your *other* reality be one of your myriad fifth-dimensional expressions of SELF. As you practice this skill in your daily life, it will become easier and easier.

Remember, the reality that you perceive, is the reality that you live.

We shall return, for we are always with you in a higher frequency,

Mytria/Mytre

Alcyone and Ashtar Command

The Beginnings of Our Ascension

MYTRIA AND MYTRE SPEAK:

Once we arrived at our new home in the Pleiades, we were finally free of war and fighting. With this freedom from fear, we could hope for a better life. We Pleiadians are so involved with our Earth Family because we totally understand the state of mind of many of you. We know how it feels to be offered hope of a new life and not be totally sure that we could trust this possibility. How could we take the risk that life could be filled with peace and calm when there had been so much war and disruption?

In fact, it took us several generations, which are longer than yours as we live much longer, to settle into the concept of the freedom to choose peace, love, happiness and joy. We understand how our dear Earth Family must decide to choose to live the hope that appears to be before you. After all, you have lived in illusion for myriad incarnations, so what if you believe in yet another illusion? At least this possible illusion is filled with multidimensional light and unconditional love. However, after living many incarnations of living in darkness and fear how can you turn away from hope?

It was the same for us. Also, we were very busy building a new life for ourselves, just as you will soon be doing. The building of our new world kept us occupied. However, the challenges of creating a new society were an ongoing challenge. For generations, we had traveled from place to place and lived entire lifetimes on Starships. Hence, our society was based on a smaller world. On the other hand, we did have long periods in which we were planet-bound, but we kept running into the same issue, again and again. We would find peace, then "they" — usually the Dracs — would find us, and the fighting would begin again.

Even though we appeared to be hidden away, there was little security as we had found "safe havens" before, only to be invaded again. Because of our many dashed hopes, we had become attached to a sense of victimization. We felt as if we had little control over the outcome of our lives, our homes and our society. Do you see why we are coming to assist our Earth Family? We are your ancestors, and we know that we are responsible for the example that we set for those who we left behind. Yes, we did abandon many of you in our constant search to find security.

Somehow, through the process of creating a new reality and having freedom from fear and victimization, we realized that what we had accused others of doing to us, we ourselves had done to others. In other words, in order to change our reality we had to change ourselves. Specifically, we had to change our state of consciousness. We had felt like "prey" for so long that we had forgotten the damage that we had done to beloved Gaia, who had twice offered us a safe home. If we did not change, and we had to do so very quickly, we would do to our new world what we had once done to Earth.

We had left our home world of Lyra to find peace, but we did not have peace within. We had fear. Finally, we were learning that we could only create in our reality what we held in our hearts and minds. This information was very difficult for us to accept. When a society is based on war and victimization for a very long time, it becomes very difficult to find the enemy within. Only those of us who had a spiritual connection could begin to look into our own darkness. Fortunately, that was enough to turn the tide of our creations.

Those of us who had remembered our connection to Spirit, began to go inside ourselves to ask for forgiveness for what we had done to others. Amazingly, we all got the same answer, but in different words. The message that we got was, "You must forgive yourself in order to accept forgiveness from another." It was one thing to ask forgiveness of our Spirit, but another thing to ask ourselves for forgiveness. First, we had to decide exactly what we needed to forgive ourselves for. We began to gather in small groups to find the answer to this question.

Fortunately, our group energy allowed us to go back into the history of our civilization in a detached fashion. Once we realized what we had done to others, we sought the answers as to why we had done these things. We realized that our sense of feeling victimized give us permission to perceive others as an enemy without adequate proof. Because of this decision-making process, we had attacked without trying to talk and abandoned without trying to heal.

This realization was a vital realization, as it became a basis of our society. Once we found that our actions were based on fear, we saw that we had gone against the very core of nature, which we had thought was based on love and acceptance. Therefore, now we needed to go back into our history and re-do our mistakes within our consciousness so that our new, habitual responses could be changed. Therefore, we reviewed our past to discern what decisions were made from a fearful stance and which decisions were based on correct perceptions of our "enemies." After we determined which ones were our fearful decisions, we re-considered how we could have used communication and healing instead.

We were able to discern situations with our Service-to-Self enemies in which we responded with powerful tactics, and the situations in which we became afraid and ran, or attacked without adequate thought. Going over our past allowed us to gain the lessons that were hidden in our "mistakes" and the wisdom that we gained from our effective choices. Once we brought this information back to our people, it became easier for them to uncover their own guilt, anger and fear. Once others experienced and released their emotions they, too, felt a need to go inside and confer with their Spirit.

First our communications with Spirit were mostly individual, but gradually small groups began to gather to release the old and feel the blessings of Spirit. The groups felt so full of Spirit that they wanted to show their joy by dancing, singing, painting, writing and many other creative expressions. The joy of expressing our creativity released a dark cloud from our consciousness that we had forgotten was there.

Suddenly, our fear and sense of victimization was gone. We were too busy creating a new life to think about fear. Since more and more of us were developing an intimate relationship with Spirit, we could surrender protection of our world and society to Spirit. We also realized that *service to others* was our greatest expression of creativity.

We were finally settling into our new home and were expanding our Galactic Duties when we began to discover a small voice within. We had started the next phase of our ascension without ever knowing that our ascension process had even begun.

We are with you always, for we share your Spirit,

Mytria/Mytre

Suzanne Lie

The Inner Voice

MYTRIA AND MYTRE CONTINUE:

We left off with the call of a *small* inner voice tickling our consciousness. After such a long time of moving, establishing, fighting and leaving we had lost most of our desire for the deep inner contemplation that had once been our keynote. Now, with peace and calm entering our lives again, we were returning to our SELF.

But, who was that voice that so many of us were hearing? Was it our Spirit in a more tangible manner, or was it a version of the SELF to whom we were returning? Some of us were too busy with their daily lives to place too much attention on these questions. On the other hand, those of a feminine, introspective expression, such as Mytria, could not ignore the questions or the inner voice. Therefore, Mytria will tell her story, as we were two people then. In fact, we had not even met.

MYTRIA SPEAKS:

I was among the ones who first banded together to connect with our Spirit, so the inner voice was not small to me. In fact, my inner voice constantly haunted me and would give me no rest. I could not sleep and ate only for survival. Therefore, I became

25

increasingly tired and eventually, sick. However, none of the healers could determine the cause of my inability to sleep, extreme sensitivity to food, aching joints, dizziness and confusion. They assumed it was because I was exhausted and recommended that I return home to rest.

However, sleep would not come. I tossed and turned and kept my housemates awake with my constant shuffling around and groaning. Finally, they came to me as one unit and suggested that I spend some time in one of the new Temples that were being created. Their suggestion brought the first inner peace I had felt since the inner voice began giving me instructions which seemed impossible to understand. In fact, it was not until the moment of my beloved friends' suggestion that I realized that I had actually been receiving instructions.

Unfortunately these instructions were in a language that I could only receive in pictures, metaphors, emotions and disassociated thoughts. Perhaps one of the Elders who were establishing the Temples could assist me. I was barely an adult, only about 70 of your years. (As I said, we live much longer than you.) I had spent most of my life on a Starship, as I was born in-between our different planetary homes. Nonetheless, since I grew up with all the stories of other worlds and was naturally VERY empathic, I felt as though I had lived through each planetary experience.

In fact, I was told that I had been with them then,

as my life seemed to run in a sequence of constant birth, death, birth, death and birth again in the same group. As a child, I remembered these lives as clearly as I remembered what I had done the day before. However, when I became an adolescent I wanted to create a NEW version of myself rather than live what appeared to be a long sequence of the same version of life over and over again.

Perhaps, my confusion and dizziness was because all my other lives were coming back to me, and all at once. Every life seemed to be telling me the same thing and leading me to the same destination. However, I could not understand what I was being told or where I was being led. I desperately needed guidance.

Because our Temples were still under construction, we had to set an appointment to talk with someone and wait for an opening. I will not use segments of years, months or days, as we counted time very differently than you do. I will just say that I was forced to wait — and suffer — for what appeared to me to be a very long time.

However, my housemates had made it quite clear that I was being a disruptive influence to our unit. They had all found their positions in creating our new life and worked day and night towards that end. I, on the other hand, had not found that which my inner voice was guiding me towards and was riddled with fearful emotions because of my inner confusion. I decided that I should go into Nature and spend my time alone in the beautiful surroundings of our new planetary home.

Consequently, the next morning before dawn, I grabbed a small "portable dwelling," which was similar to your "tents," packed some staples and simple cookware and took off into the woods. I had no idea where I was going or what I was going to do. Yet, as I left my message for my housemates as to my destination, I felt a brief, very brief, moment of peace. Then I quietly left, closing the door on my first experience of a planetary home.

Since I had grown up visiting new planets, moons and asteroids, my survival skills in an unknown terrain were excellent. I never thought for a moment that I would be in any danger. Besides that, I had always had an attachment to the land of any area that we visited. In fact it was my guidance, along with others', that assisted us to find this beautiful world of abundance and peace. I had no idea where I was going, but I was a born navigator and knew I could return to our small village when it was time for my appointment.

I walked all day before I found a sheltered place where I could put up my dwelling. With my dwelling constructed, I sat down to eat some of the simple food that I had quietly packed. I only brought enough food for a few meals, as I did not want to take from my dear friends. Besides, I was quite confident that I could live off the land. As I ate, looking out into the ever-darkening sky, I felt calmer than I had been since my inner voice had started screaming in my mind. The food actually tasted good, and I enjoyed every bite. Surely, this was a sign that I had made the right choice.

Surprisingly, I woke up to the first storm we had experienced since we landed on this planet. I awoke clutching a small blanket and realized that my dwelling had blown away and my eating utensils where scattered all over the area. Some of them I never found. I had wanted an adventure, but I got a bit more than I had counted on. I knew better than to walk around in a storm, so I took what I could gather and huddled under the lip of an overhanging rock.

As I sat against the rock I mused. I had walked since before dawn and only stopped when it grew dark. Then, I stayed up until late watching the new star systems in the night sky. I can only imagine it was because I had been so tired that I did not see any of the warning signs for this huge storm. And, why did I not wake up sooner? Perhaps I had lived in Starships too long, and I had lost touch with nature. It definitely appeared that I had lost touch with myself.

Since the stars were now invisible, and they were the form of navigation that I had learned on the Starship, I had to stay put until the storm ended and the skies cleared. Only the great fatigue that I had been experiencing for many rotations of our moons could allow me to fall asleep in the midst of a huge storm. I do not know how long I slept, or if it was actually sleep, as my mind was seeing that which had up until now evaded me. I remember repeatedly saying in my night body, "I must remember this dream."

I awoke to a beautifully clear day with that thought in my mind. However, I could not remember the dream. I only had the same flitting images that had been haunting me since the voice began. However, the dream seemed to place these images in a sequence, which—of course—I could not remember. A great light that was shinning on my body, drying my clothes and warming the rock had awakened me. I was lying back against the rock that had offered me shelter from the storm when something caught my attention. When I looked more closely, I saw that the rock glistened as if a million small stars were embedded within it.

I had been to many planets and seen many landscapes, but I had never seen a rock like this before. I decided that since the storm had brought me here, I would stay here, against this rock for as long as necessary. However, what was left of my food was gone, so I had to remember my empathic skills of finding water and of "knowing" what is edible. It was these innate abilities that had brought me purpose on the Starship, a purpose that I had lost since we had settled into our new world. The water was found, the food was located, the night skies were mapped and I was—useless.

Perhaps that is one of the reasons why I had been having so much difficulty. I had not found my place within our society. I was too young to serve in the Temples and too old to sit around, which is what

I had been doing. No wonder my housemates had tired of my presence. With the thought of my inability to find my "place" I drifted off into sleep—or was it a deep meditation?

We shall return and Mytria will continue her story,

Mytria/Mytre

The Sacred Rock

MYTRIA CONTINUES HER STORY:

I appeared to awaken, only to see my physical form hunched against a huge rock, clutching a few possessions. As I looked at my physical self I could see how her inner conflict had robbed her of her beauty and made her body overly thin and pale. In fact, I could see how she was very sick and in great need of healing. However, it was not her body that was ill, it was her mind. I went over to her sleeping form and touched her head. Instantly, the look on her face relaxed and her breathing became long and rhythmic. Now, it was safe for me to leave her.

I, the part of her SELF with whom she has not yet connected, recognized the rock immediately. The rock was a Sacred Rock, a Portal into the realms of the higher frequencies of reality within the planet. I stood before the rock and allowed my spiritual essence to breathe into it, as I toned with my etheric voice. Slowly the Sacred Rock began to glow brighter and brighter. Gradually, a circular pattern began to glow inside the small area that served as a roof for my physical form.

The circular pattern pulled in my breath and beckoned me to tone louder and louder. My voice did not awaken my sleeping form as it was unheard by her physical ears. However, the Rock heard me, and the Portal responded by opening. My etheric essence flowed into the Portal, which transported me into the *Heart of the Planet*. Within this Heart were many other etheric forms that had physical forms on the surface.

One of these etheric ones was of a male essence. We were instantly drawn to each other, and when we touched it was as though we merged. We were quite happy with this degree of intimacy. In fact, without words, we let each other know that our joining felt natural and extremely nurturing. Then, our attention was drawn away from each other as a huge being of Light entered the Circle that we, the etheric beings, had not realized we had formed. My new friend and I both recognized him/her as an Arcturian.

The Arcturian stepped into the Center of our Circle and reached out an arm of light to introduce a beaming Light of somewhat humanoid form. This Being was of a feminine energy pattern, and she introduced herself as the Elohim for Alcyone. Even though I had never heard the word, Alcyone, I instantly knew it was the name of the binary Star System of our new planet. I will endeavor to repeat what she expressed. I did not know that my physical self could not have understood these words, as they were in the Light Language that had evaded my physical expression's understanding.

A New Home

ELOHIM ALCYONE SPEAKS:

"Beloved etheric representations of my new humanoid family, I welcome you to enjoy the beauty and fertility of one of my planetary forms. The Arcturian and I have been sending messages into the consciousness of those who could hear us. You are now here in your etheric form, as your dense bodies have been unable to hear my call and are unable to enter into the core of my planets. The one whose form is known as Mytria has discovered my "front door," and the rest of you are here while your physical forms are meditating or sleeping.

The Arcturian and I wish to tell you that you are on the cusp of a great opportunity, for this planet is about to ascend into its fifth-dimensional expression. If you can maintain a deep heart-connection to me while my planet makes this transition, you can join me in your multidimensional expression of form. Once, you have gained that form you can wear whatever frequency of body that suits your needs. You will lose nothing by this alteration and will gain a great deal.

However, the process of this transmutation is not for the weak of heart, the lazy or those who lack the quality of deep commitment. It was no accident that you have arrived on this planetary body, as I have chosen you to be my Keepers. The Arcturians and I have watched you for many of your generations and have constantly been within your consciousness since you first landed here.

We have sent an open call to those who are willing to assist this planet with its transition. In return, I will assist you. The Arcturians will assist us both, as personal and planetary ascension is their Cosmic Service. We wish you to look around at the etheric forms of those in this meeting, for YOU are the ones who have shown the greatest dedication and commitment to creating a new reality based on multidimensional light and unconditional love.

You will likely forget those you see here now, as that is by design. We want you all to connect as ONE Light-force within your etheric body and to ground your personal and group commitment into the body of this planet when you return to your daily life. When you meet each other in your physical realm, you will feel a certain twinge in your heart and recognition in your mind. However, you will not know each other as you see each other now until the transformation of this planetary body has been completed.

I thank you for finding your way here. I deeply appreciate it, as I have seen the difficult initiations that you have all completed in order to find your way to this gathering. You are my Protectors and the Keepers of my Flame. I KNOW that you shall find your way to our next gathering, and we will meet again at the completion of your personal and planetary ascension.

Until then, know that I AM forever within and about you. I AM the Creator Mother of the planet upon which you stand and from which you eat, drink and bathe. Therefore, I AM the land that gives you a home, the water that is vital for your life force and the fire that warms your homes and ignites your passion for life. I AM the air that you breathe and the skies through which you will fly your ever-transforming Starships.

I welcome you to my Planet, soon to be an ascended member of my Star System.

I welcome you to MY body and MY Soul.

We, the Arcturians and I, are in constant communication with you. As I complete my message, the Arcturians will give a personal message to each of you. Therefore, line up one-by-one to *accept your personal message.*

I, Alcyone, will not leave you, for I AM within you!"

As the Elohim Alcyone said the last sentence, her light disbursed in every direction. It went into the ceiling of our Inner Cave, into the walls, the floor, the many alcoves, and into the etheric form of each of us. For a moment, I felt in complete unity with the planet, and in complete unity with the stranger with whom I has mysteriously connected. However, the light of the Elohim told us, "not yet," and our connection was severed.

We were almost embarrassed as we lined up for our personal message. He allowed me to stand before him, and I felt as if my heart was broken. What was that connection? Who was that person? Last, but not least, would I ever meet him again?

Mytria

A New Home

Merging of Divine Complements
PART II

The Cave

MYTRIA CONTINUES:

I am embarrassed to say that I vividly remembered the feeling of the merging with the male etheric form to the tiniest detail, but I could not remember my personal message from The Arcturian. Was I that desperate for love that I would disrespect the message that was given me directly from an Arcturian? Fortunately, I did not ponder that question when I first awoke. I was too weak. My etheric form had stayed out of my body for too long, and my body was going into shock.

I experienced two realities at once. I felt my etheric body desperately trying to get back into my physical shell, and I also felt my weak, cold and semi-conscious physical form try to accept its spirit. I was not dreaming or even meditating. I had a high fever and my body was turning blue. I was barely breathing and I was very, very cold.

I pulled myself into a tight ball and pushed against the rock in an urgent and futile attempt to find warmth. I kept loosing consciousness, coming back, then passing out again. It would soon be dark, and the nights were very cold here. I don't know if I was conscious or unconscious when I saw a beautiful Lady of Light. She was huge and looked as though she was made of clouds and stars. I called to her to help me as she floated towards me. I don't know if the next memory was real or a hallucination, but she floated right past me and into the rock against which I was leaning.

Blessed warmth seemed to stream from where she entered the rock, and I heard a haunting lyrical tone in my mind. Somehow I found the strength to crawl towards the place where the Light Being entered the rock. I was so weak that I had to hold on to the rock to stand up, but when I did so, I fell through a slit, or was it the vortex, and into a dark cave. It was warm, and I heard running water as I fell off to sleep.

I don't know how long I slept, but I do remember stirring to drink some water, then going back to sleep. After a while, I discovered some fungus growing by the water. I brought a piece of it to my nose and lips and sensed that it was fine to eat. I took just a few bites, then fell back to sleep, completely full.

Finally, I woke up feeling restless and saw what looked like a beam of light. Holding onto the wall of the cave to rise and to walk, I followed the beam of light to its source, which was the mouth of the cave. The air was clear and warm, and I felt better than I had in a long time. I had almost forgotten my "dream, meditation and/or vision," but I remembered that the planet was beautiful and fertile.

I dozed in the Sun until hunger stirred me to find some edible plants and roots. The water that ran through the cave gathered in a small pond outside the cave that was surrounded by plants. I recognized several plants as edible and found my one remaining bowl, filled it with water and drank while I ate the plants. When it grew cold, I went back into the cave to sleep. I'm not sure how long I lived like this, for I was so deep within my self that I often did not note the passage of days.

I lived in the now of nature. I ate when I was hungry, drank when I was thirsty, moved when I was stiff and slept when I was tired. I was outside when the weather permitted and in the cave when it was cold, raining or dark. However, sometimes I stayed up very late or got up very early to memorize stars and constellations. Then when I was stronger, I began to wander the land to map that, as well.

I grew healthier every day and slept soundly every night. My dreams were very vivid, but I usually forgot them in the light of day. I did not try to hold them in my memory. In fact, I did not "try" to DO anything. I lived with the land, looked up into the sky, soaked in the pond and rummaged for food. One day I found two rocks that created a spark when struck again each other, and I was able to make a fire.

In order for me to move forward into my greater expression of self, I went backward into the primitive elements of survival. After a while, even the memory of my merging with the male was lost from my memory. I could not think about what had happened before or what would happen next. I lived every breath in calm serenity. I think I could have lived my entire life that way, until I met him.

I had traveled very far that day and had found a wonderful lake with a waterfall and a lovely place to dive into the deep water. After my small pond, it was exhilarating to dive, swim and stand beneath the waterfall. I was having such a delightful time that I did not notice that night was approaching. Finally, I looked up and realized that I must hurry back to the cave. I climbed out of the water and was walking quickly toward the direction of my cave when I ran directly into someone.

I could not see his face in the dim light, but I knew instantly that it was him! It was the male with whom I had merged in the cave. But now he was physical, and so was I.

When we return, Mytre will speak of his early awakening.

Mytria/Mytre

Recognition

MYTRE SPEAKS:

"Where have you been?" I spoke gruffly, perhaps to cover up the intensity of emotion that I felt at her very touch. "Your friends are concerned for you and sent me to find you." I said in a softer voice.

"How do you know that I am the one you seek?" she replied with a resonance in her voice that instantly calmed my demeanor.

"I am sorry I was so gruff with you. It is just that I have been searching for you such a very long time. How did you get lost way out here?"

"I am not lost. I live close by."

"Live?" I said trying to control my intense emotions. "There is no where to live out here."

"Follow me," she said. "I will show you my home."

She walked away, and I followed her without question. We walked through almost total darkness, but never hesitated. As I followed her strangely familiar form I became more and more enchanted by her. Who was she? Why did I feel like I knew her? I had never had these feelings for anyone in my life, and I had barely seen her face.

We walked for quite a while in total silence, while I tried to contain my emotions and see in the darkness. The moons had not come up yet and the sky was hazy, yet her every step was sure as if she had made this journey many times. Meanwhile, I was trying to maintain my dignity and not trip or fall. I, who took such pride in being a leader, followed her every footstep.

As if timed by some unseen source, the moons came up just as we came around a huge rock and entered a small area filled with flowers, plants, a small pond and even flat rocks that were arranged like chairs. How did she move those rocks? However, I said nothing. I did not want to embarrass myself again by speaking rashly. However, obviously she was NOT lost, and I had greatly misjudged her.

"It is getting cold now. Would you like to come inside?" she said as if she totally trusted me.

"Ah, yes," I stammered in a very undignified manner.

"Let me start a fire, so you can see inside," she said as she moved to a collection of rocks that created a small fire pit just outside the cave in a small, sheltered area. She collected some kindling and what looked like moss, struck two stones together, and instantly a small flame ignited the kindling. She had obviously lit this fire many times. Then she took what looked like a grid and placed it onto the rocks.

"I will make some tea to warm us." She easily said.

"You have tea?" I said in a rudely, surprised

manner.

"Oh yes," she said as she guided mc into the cave where I saw many herbs hanging upside-down to dry.

"Where did you find these?" I asked, again in a voice that was too surprised.

She ignored my rude behavior and turned towards me to reply. However, when our eyes met in the flickering light, neither one of us could speak for what seemed to be forever. It was she who spoke first.

"I know you," she said without any shyness.

"Yes." was all I could say. I did know her, but I also knew I had never met her.

She turned again and chose some herbs, broke them up and put them into a small metal pan. She filled the pan with water from the clear creek that trickled through the cave and placed the pan on the grid.

"Would you like honey?" she said.

"You have honey?"

She smiled in response to my question.

"Sure." I stammered again.

Rather than embarrass myself further, I looked around the small cave to get my bearings and to calm down. I could not believe my eyes. She had, indeed, created a home here, and she appeared to be alone.

"Do you live alone here?"

"Oh no! I am not alone. I live with Nature."

I glanced around her home again. Off to the

right I saw what was likely her bedding. It looked old and well used.

"Yes, I see that you do. I am sorry for my rudeness. I have greatly underestimated you. I expected to find you wounded, or worse, and in great danger. Instead, I see that you have created a lovely home. How did you do all this?"

"I asked the Great Mother for help." She said, as if I would know what that meant.

"The Great Mother?"

"Yes, you know the Elohim Alcyone who we met in the Core."

"But, that was just a dream. How could you know about my dream?"

In fact, I was quite surprised that the "dream" instantly returned to my memory.

She chose to completely ignore my question and turned to create a small meal comprised of food that I had never seen. She took two half-gourds, which she used for plates and guided me to a small ledge. In front of the ledge was a small table made of intertwined twigs.

In complete amazement, I sat where she indicated and silently watched while she put the plates on the "table" and went to gather the tea.

"I am afraid I only have one cup. Do you mind if we share?"

I silently nodded my head in amazement, as she handed me the tea.

"Oh," she said as she walked over to another ledge where she had a small metal container. She

Suzanne Lie

brought it back and offered it to me saying,

"Would you like some of this honey?"

Again I silently nodded, as she poured a small amount of the sweet liquid into the steaming tea.

"Please eat," she said and offered me my plate.

"I don't want to be rude," I said too late, as I had already been incredibly rude, "but how do you know that these plants are not poisonous?"

"They told me." She simply replied.

"Uh, how did they tell you?" I questioned.

"I merely smelled them and placed them on my heart. If they were poisonous, I felt fear, and if they were nutritious I felt love."

"But wasn't that dangerous? What if you were wrong?"

"I trusted myself, and I trusted Nature."

I said nothing more. I shared the delicious tea and ate the tasty plants. I guess if she could trust me enough to bring me into her home, I could trust her enough to eat her food. Trust? I pondered that concept, as I tried to think of the last time that I had trusted anyone.

Mytria's awakening happened before we met, whereas my awakening started that evening. Everything that had been important in my life seemed unimportant compared to the simple peace that she shared with me that first night. I had been driven by ambition and trusted no one in my struggle to become a leader and Protector in our new world.

Interestingly, so many people trusted me, but I

47

trusted no one. However, I did trust her. I ate her possibly poisonous food and drank her tea of an unknown "herb" without hesitation. In fact, as I sat on that small ledge, I knew that my life had changed forever. I would never be the same person again, which was a good thing. I had not been too fond of myself lately.

As if reading my mind, she looked into my eyes and said, "I was nearly dead when I came here. The Mother has healed me and has given me a wonderful life."

She then took the plates and our one-cup and went outside to wash them. I said nothing and didn't even offer to help her. I had come here to save her, but it was apparent that it was she who would save me.

I, Mytre, will return to continue my story...

Suzanne Lie

Unity

MYTRE CONTINUES:

We slept together in the small alcove with her worn bedding. However, she had put something underneath it, and it was incredible warm and soft. She slept as soundly and sweetly as a baby. I of course, slept very little at all. My mind would not stop. Everything that I had ever believed in, all the structure, lessons, discipline and obedience that I had grown up with had been revealed as the old paradigm for my past life.

As l lay there with her warm body next to mine, in fact, VERY close to mine, I knew that I was changed forever. I had no idea what I had changed into, but I was positive that the "me" I used to be had died a sudden death. As I lay in the warm darkness with the scent of her body filling my heart, I reviewed my life. I was born to a military family. There was no choice as to what I would do. Of course, I would be a military person. It was our family's legacy to protect our world, our way of life.

However, since we came to this planet, our reality had vastly changed. For the first time in my life, which was about 90 of your years, making me a young adult, I did not KNOW what my life would be. Now that our people were able to "let their guard down" and "feel safe in their new home," my important contribution of being a protector was not so important. However, as I saw others settling down and totally changing their perspective on life, I held strongly to the indoctrination that I had since birth.

Maybe I was a unique person, and maybe I could find a unique experience of life that was different from all the generations of our *proud and brave heritage*. That kind of thinking had been hidden in my brain since I was a small child. Since childhood, I had never allowed those thoughts to come to the surface. Then, I literally ran into a woman and experienced her entirely unique experience of life. It was then that those hidden childhood thoughts began prying their way to the surface.

How could I possibly push aside all that I had stood for, all that I thought defined me as a powerful man, and all that I thought I loved? Now, in one very long night, I had become a totally different person. However, I did not know this new person, so I had no idea who I was or what I would do. I only knew that I could not go back to our village in this state of confusion.

As if she had heard my thoughts, Mytria rolled over to face me with opened eyes and smiled. Now there was no question. Not only could I not return to a life that had become barren of meaning, I could not leave that smile.

Mytria quietly got up and started her small fire. I watched as she put water in her small pan to make OUR tea, then went outside, likely to wash. Without her next to me, I felt lonely. How could that be? I had just met her, but it felt like we had always been together.

While she was gone, I went to my pack and got my communication device. However, it did not work here. Perhaps it is the cave, I thought as I rose to go outside to use it. Before she even turned around, she said, "Your device won't work here. There is an etheric shield around this area, and no technology works here. Believe me, I tried." When she turned toward me to continue speaking I experienced that same feeling of recognition, and any doubts I had about staying vanished.

"You have decided to stay?"

"Do you always read my thoughts?" I asked with a smile in my voice.

"Only when you are thinking about me," she smiled in return. "Are you avoiding my question?"

"Yes," I said. "I was thinking that I should ask you first."

"Yes!"

"Yes I should ask you, or yes I should stay?"

"Yes, I would love to get to know you and show you my world."

"I will have to tell them that you are safe and I am not returning—yet."

"Then you will destroy that device?"

I had not thought of making my decision so

permanent, so unalterable, but I realized that the kind of change I was facing would take my total commitment.

"Yes."

"Would you like to help me find some eggs? I will ask the birds if they can surrender one for us."

After we had eaten the surrendered eggs and more delicious plants, which she had seasoned with her unknown herbs, she showed me the portal out of the energy field and turned to go back to her home.

"Aren't you going with me to make sure that I destroy the device?" I teasingly said.

"I trust you." She said as she turned away.

ΔΔΔΔ

Her trust was the most amazing part of my experience. Not only did she totally trust me, which she said was because she knew me, she also totally trusted Nature. She lived her every moment in unity with the planet and the flora and fauna which whom she shared her life. There was no differentiation between what was alive and what was a *thing*. Everything, even a rock, was alive in her world.

I wanted to share her world, but my scientific mind rebelled at such novel thinking. I had never realized how indoctrinated I was until I tried to change my mind. On the other hand, my body showed no resistance to change. I quickly forgot about my uniform and only wore what I normally slept in. The weather was usually quite hot in the day and cold at night, but our bed was always warm.

When it was not too cold, we would sleep outside and she would show me all the Star Systems she had found. I was able to fill in many of the official names, but I usually preferred her names for them. In the day, we took long walks so that she could show me all the territory she had mapped. I assisted her with that. There was a plant that grew by a nearby river, which she had learned to "beat" into a kind of paper and she would write on it with "ink" which was sap from a certain tree.

Other plants could be dried and woven into a cloth, of which she made me an amazingly comfortable garment. She also showed me where all the eatable plants were, as well as the source of her honey. She showed me how to be so still that a bird would land on my shoulder and so quiet that I could hear the beating of my heart.

Fortunately, I was not useless. I had the strength that she lacked and a few tools, which allowed us to make our home even more comfortable. Yes, it was OUR home. We lived in it as one person, sharing all chores without any conflict or duty. If something needed to be done, we did it. However, we had our specialties. If we needed something built or moved, I was called in. On the other hand, if we needed to consult the Mother, she was called in.

Then one day she told me that it was time for me become ONE with the Mother Planet. I told her that I had no idea how to do that, and quite frankly, I did not think the Mother wanted to become ONE with me.

"How can you say that?" she said in a shocked voice.

"I am not pure, like you. I have killed many beings and destroyed much land. I have been a warrior where the love that you speak of is a weakness and the trust that you hold is mere foolishness."

"Do YOU feel that way?"

I had to think before I answered her. She deserved a true response, and I did not know my truth yet. Hence, all I could say was, "I did feel that way once, but that me is no-more. I don't know this new me enough to answer your question. I do believe you, and I see the great strength that you have gained not by domination, but through surrender. However, I don't think it is possible for me to connect with something as vague as the Great Mother."

"You do not need to surrender to Her, for I am Her representative. Therefore, you can surrender to me. It is often that way with men. Their minds are filled with protection and duty. Only deep love with a woman can allow them to release their protections and totally surrender."

"How did you know that I deeply love you? I don't even think I knew it myself until you said the words."

Without a word spoken, she took me into our cave to give me the "proof" I needed.

As we merged through our love making, our

consciousness intermingled so deeply that I could feel how she communed with all life. With this feeling shared between us, she showed me how to touch the land to find water, to smell a plant and put it to my heart to determine if it was safe to eat, how to ask a bird to surrender an egg, how to read the weather long before it changed, and how to look into my SELF.

"Your relationship with the Mother depends on your relationship with your SELF." She told me again and again. At first, the relationship with my SELF could only come as a by-product of my relationship with her. I had never been taught to have a relationship with my SELF. I was taught to follow orders, fulfill my duty and obey my commanding officers. I had spent my life being the "effect" of an external "cause." If I was successful in my endeavor, I was happy and proud of myself. If I failed in my duty, I was ashamed and angry with myself.

I had not heard of the "greater" or "higher" version of my SELF that Mytria spoke of. The only greater part of me would be my fellow warriors, and my higher self was my commanding officers. I lived on the outside of me. Inside of me were bones and blood and organs that somehow survived their myriad wounds. I had no concept of a spirit me, or the etheric me with whom Mytria said she had merged within the Core. In fact, I had no concept of that experience other than it being a "sexy" dream.

However, I had finally trusted someone. I

trusted Mytria absolutely and completely. I trusted that she could make my energies rise up from my spine into my heart, or even into my mind. However, I had no faith that I could accomplish this without her help. It was this concept that disturbed me greatly. Was I becoming hypnotized by someone who was showing me a vision of reality that could never be mine?

Again, she read my thoughts. "I think you have had enough for now. It is time for you to go on a vision quest."

"A vision quest, what is that?" I said in an angry fashion. She has tired of being my teacher, as I had become weak in her eyes. This entire experience was a fantasy, an excuse to ignore my duties. What had I been thinking? How could I dare to be different than all the men in as many generations as I could count? A vision quest, HA, get out of my home is more like it.

Mytria did not engage in my inner battle. She merely turned and went into the cave.

Vision Quest

MYTRE CONTINUES:

When Mytria turned away without even answering my question and walked into the cave I was enraged. Who did she think I was, some toy that she could play with and discard when I became boring? Without another thought I turned and walked away as fast as I could. In fact, walking was not fast enough, so I began to run. I had not realized what good condition I was in from my time on the land, but I did not become fatigued until it was almost sunset.

The running felt good; it felt real. Also, I was proud of myself that I didn't stay there and humble myself even further. I had been following her around like a child long enough. I was a MAN, a protector who had a bright future in the military. How could I have become so lost, so ensnared in the trap of a woman's arms? I guess it was time to go back to being myself. This time had been a fun fantasy, but it was time for reality, for duty.

I continued to walk at a very rapid pace as the sun continued to move below the horizon. I was so engaged in my anger, self-pity, and (I hate to admit it) fear, that I was not paying any attention to the land. In my effort to forget about Mytria, I was trying to forget everything she had shown me. Then it happened…

I did not even notice how close I was standing to a huge precipice, nor did I notice the loose rocks under my feet. Then, before I could come out of my self-pity, I began to fall. Fortunately, the rocks tumbled beneath me so I did not drop straight down, but I could see a steep ledge coming up below me. If I went over that ledge I would be gravely injured or die. I grabbed desperately at the surrounding roots and plants, but they all broke off with my grasp.

Finally, I got hold of a large enough root to bear my weight, but not for long. I had to find a way to land on that ledge, but it was over to my right. The surrounding cliff was loose rock so I would have to create a *controlled fall* like I had learned in the military. Perhaps I could swing from the root so that I would fall onto the ledge, but I had to avoid the loose rocks. I had to decide NOW, as the root was giving way.

I focused my attention and intention on the destination of my *fall*, swung the root a bit to the right and jumped/fell. I did land on the ledge, but with such force that I felt my right leg break beneath me. I almost lost my balance, but somehow leaned against the wall of the ledge until I felt secure. I carefully sat down to assess the condition of my leg.

I was only wearing the short robe, tied at the waist with a sash, which Mytria had made me from her plant material. The very thought of her name brought not anger, but overwhelming grief. What had I done? Why had I become so angry? No, the proper question was, why had I become so afraid? However, this was not the time to ponder my erratic behavior. This was the time to think about my survival. I had only the clothes on my back. Some military man I was to run off into the wilderness with no supplies, not even a knife.

I pulled myself over to some long sticks, put them on both sides of my leg and wrapped my sash around them to somewhat steady my leg. I would have to find a way to set it myself, if I lived that long. There was only a dim light and it was becoming cold already. I had to protect my body from going into shock. There was only a small ledge and loose dirt around me. Therefore, I dug myself into the surrounding dirt, leaving out my leg to avoid infection. I had no food, no water, no supplies and no tools. Furthermore, I had totally lost all touch with Nature and had no idea where I was.

All I could do now was sleep so that my body could begin to heal itself. I would have to control my mind and calm my breathing. I felt the adrenaline coursing through my body, which would keep me alert, when what I needed was to remain calm. My wound was not fatal unless it got infected, which was a huge possibility in these circumstances. I would have to ask the Mother for help.

Did I actually have that thought?

It was in that exact moment that I had the first experience of my "Higher Self." I knew that my brain had that thought, but it was not the same brain that hysterically ran off like a frightened dog.

"Do not judge yourself," came an unbidden thought.

And then, I had the most amazing experience of unconditional love, at least it seemed that way. Perhaps it was Mytria, for she was the only one in my life that made me feel that way.

"NO, it is I," continued the inner voice.

I had heard about the inner voice before. In response to this voice some people totally changed their lives and became very spiritual, whereas others became sick, confused, angry and frightened when they heard it. I realized then that I had been in the later group. I had been unable to perceive any form of inner world. Even during my time with Mytria, I could not communicate with the Mother Planet who was underneath and around me.

Never before had I imagined another reality within me. I only thought about and attended to the physical world. With these last words, with this last thought, I started to drift off into sleep. At least, I thought it was sleep. Maybe it was a hallucination, or maybe I was dying. However, now I know that it was the Truth.

"Truth"—that was a word that was just as dubious as the word Trust. I had trusted Mytria, totally and without question. Why had the mere suggestion of a Vision Quest sent me into such an emotional state? That question was the last thought I had before I passed out, went to sleep, or had a Vision!

In my vision, I was alone on the land. It was the same land that I had shared with Mytria, but it was filled with light. Everything had a soft aura around it and seemed to whisper to me as I passed by.

I too had a glow around me, and my body seemed to be made of light. It appeared to be almost transparent. I looked down to see if my leg was healed and found that, yes, it was totally fine, but my feet were not totally touching the ground. I was moving in a walking, floating motion, almost like treading water in our wonderful lake.

Again a pang of overwhelming grief overtook me, and I bolted into consciousness. What have I done? How could I have ruined the only good thing in my life? Why was I so afraid that she was tired of me?

"Because you were tired of yourself," came that damned voice.

Then, I realized that I had damned my own inner voice, my own self. Suddenly, I began to realize all the ways that I had damned myself throughout my entire life. Finally, I realized that I do NOT like killing.

I do not like killing other people, I do not like destroying their homes or disrupting their property. I do not like destroying anything or anyone. I don't want to be a destroyer. I thought I would grow up to be a Protector, but instead I became an enemy of people and beings that were "different" from me — but were they really different?

They all had a heart or maybe two, they all had brains, many had much larger brains than mine, and they ALL had families. AND, I had destroyed them, as well as their families. How could I ever forgive myself? How could I ever be the person that I saw in my Vision? Yes, it was a Vision. At least I could own that.

"It is not a Vision, it is the Truth," I heard inside.

"What Truth, the truth that I was a destroyer or the truth that I was having a vision?" Now, I was arguing with my inner voice.

"The Truth is that you ARE the person that you saw in your Vision," whispered the voice within.

After that I think I passed out. However, I did awaken with those final words of "You ARE the person that you saw." Yes, amazingly enough, these words, this Truth, was still in my heart, right next to my love for Mytria. That thought jarred me fully awake to a mid-day sun. I pulled myself out of the dirt and started to take a military assessment of my situation, when I felt Mytria's love.

Even though, I had fallen off a cliff to avoid her love, it was right where it had ALWAYS been. It was the love she had for me that had forced me to find the love I had for myself. Therefore, I pushed aside my old way of being. After all, it was that combative attitude that had gotten me into this fix. Then, my Protector self came into play. I had to protect Mytria, but I had to stay alive to do so.

"What about the planet? Do you have to protect Her too?"

It appeared that even when I was totally conscious and in broad daylight, the inner voice was still active. Did I have the courage to listen to it?

Under Starry Skies

MYTRIA SPEAKS:

When Mytre ran away from me, I was sure my heart would break. When I mentioned the Vision Quest I had spoken from within, without hesitation. And now, I have lost him. How could I have used such harsh words? I spent the rest of the day inside the cave feeling worse than I could ever remember. How could I go from such wonderful heights of ecstasy and then plummet into deep despair? Had I lost all touch with my inner peace just because I had lost a man? However, he was not just any man. He was my Divine Complement, my Twin Flame. That is what the inner voice said, and my heart agreed.

I tortured myself through the entire day and into sunset, when I suddenly had a feeling of deep urgency and pending disaster. Something was about to happen or had just happened to Mytre. I calmed my mind and went inside to speak to the Mother. All I heard was "Send him healing love." Then, I became terrified for that clearly meant that he was injured. But, where was he injured, and how? It was too late to follow his tracks, as I would only get lost myself. All I could do was spend most of the night worrying.

Then, I heard the Mother saying, "Drink some calming tea and sleep. You must be alert for tomorrow." I did what she said and finally fell into a fitful sleep. I do not remember any dreams, nor did I get much rest. However, I woke up knowing that he had been injured, and I knew that I must find him. At sunrise, I packed all my healing herbs, poultices, more clothes, food and water. My pack was heavy, and I would not able to run. Therefore, I had to bring some kindling and my firestones. He had walked off in the direction where the forest ended, and there would be nothing to burn.

As soon as it was light enough I started my journey. My pack was heavy and I had to go slowly to read his tracks. Sometimes there seemed to be no tracks, and I had to stop to consult the Mother. I walked all day and almost till dark. I had never been to this area, so I had to stop and set up camp. There would be no use in both of us becoming injured. After I had eaten a small meal, I tried to go within, but my growing fear for his safety did not allow me any information or much sleep.

MYTRE SPEAKS:

It was mid-day, and I had to find a way to get off this ledge. Another night in the cold without food or water would be far too dangerous for my leg. I had not noticed the large gash in my leg, which was now infected, and I knew I had a fever. If I didn't move, I would pass out again. I had to trust the Inner Voice. I could not abandon Mytria in this way, I could not abandon my duty, and I could not abandon my self.

As I looked around, I could see no means of escape. Therefore, I looked inside to ask the Inner Voice. Perhaps I was hallucinating, but as soon as I closed my eyes, I saw the image of my SELF in my Vision Quest. "Follow me and listen to the Mother," he said as he moved along the ledge to my right. I would have to crawl and drag my right leg, as I could not damage it more by putting weight on it.

After what seemed like forever, I found a space between the edge of the ledge and a bolder that I could—very carefully—crawl along. Once I went around the bolder, I found a gentler incline toward the top. The ground here was more stable, and there was even some foliage to grab onto. The Inner Voice reminded me to listen to the Mother again, and so I did. I touched the earth in the manner that Mytria had taught me and asked for Her guidance.

Instantly, I had a feeling to follow a certain trough in the earth, which afforded me enough security to frequently rest. I fought off my dizziness from my fever and lack of water, and contacted the Mother with my every choice of movement. My progress was very slow, but I was gradually moving up the side of the cliff. However, it was getting dark. I had to get to the top while there was enough light to see what I was doing.

I realized that I was going slowly for the sake of my leg, but I had to move more quickly to reach the top before dark. I closed my eyes for a moment to remember my vision. This version of me could move without even touching the ground. If I could

BE that me, then I could trust my every movement without hesitation. It took a while to envision myself in that manner, but I gradually began to feel a light about my form. I slowly opened my eyes to see that my body and the cliff around me were glowing.

I pushed aside my doubts of "hallucination" and chose to believe my experience. Now, I knew exactly where to place my hands and my good leg. There was no hesitation, no fear, no adrenalin, and no pain. I was in some sort of trance that allowed me to become ONE with the cliff. It almost felt as if the cliff was assisting my movement. When I looked up and saw an overhanging ledge, I did not fear.

Instead, I swiftly found an alternate route that allowed me to easily crawl over the top and onto flat ground. I rolled away from the cliff and I pulled myself over to a huge rock that held the heat of the day. I pushed myself against the warm rock and patted it to thank the Mother. Then, I looked up into the starry sky under which Mytria and I had fallen asleep many times and saw my body of light embracing hers. With this image in my mind, I fell into a deep sleep.

MYTRIA AND MYTRE SPEAK:

We realized later that we were very close to each other, but did not know it. However, this physical distance was necessary for us to bridge the etheric gap that still existed between us. We both looked into the starry sky and thanked the Mother for assisting us. Even though our bodies were apart, our hearts and minds were joined as we fell asleep. In fact, we had the same dream, or was it a vision?

We found ourselves back in the Core of the Mother, at the exact moment of our "accidental" merging. Now, after all we had been through, being merged into one person felt even stronger. We were both different people now. We had both survived and successfully completed our initiations and had conquered our inner demons, which made our love even stronger.

As we stood as one, looking into each other's eyes, the Mother came to us. We thought it was to bless us, but it was actually to give us our next assignment.

"My beloved children," She said to us both, "You may think your long journey has ended, but it has actually just begun. I need you both to help me, as you have both become my allies of transmutation. You have transformed yourselves, and now I must ask you to assist me to transmute my Planet."

We were both deeply honored, but somehow worried. Was there something in Her voice that made us concerned that we could not stay together? NO, we would not allow that to happen. After all we had been through; we would never part again— NEVER!

We both awoke to the hint of dawn. There was not enough light for Mytria to read the tracks, but we were joined into one being again. Therefore, she simply followed the call of my love. It was midday when we rejoined again.

MYTRE SPEAKS:

When I awoke from my dream/vision, I knew Mytria was near. I touched the land to call her via the earth and sent my love out to her direction. In fact, I could see in my mind exactly where she was, just as she told me later that she could see me in the same way. I pulled myself up the hill a bit so that I could more easily see her approach. I found a strong stick and somehow got myself to my feet. I would not greet her lying on the ground like a wounded animal.

It was then that I saw her walking towards me. When she saw me, she laid down her heavy pack and ran to me as fast as she could. When we met, our hearts burst with the love that we thought we had lost, only to regain—stronger than ever. We held each other so tight that we seemed to be one body, as Mytria sobbed onto my chest. I tried not to cry, but my joy could only be expressed in that manner.

We stood there for a long time. All my pain was temporarily gone with the merging of our bodies. In fact, I felt a great healing force coming from her and into my body. As she held me and wept, I felt my fever diminish and my leg begin to heal. Then I realized that she was draining herself too much in her effort to heal me. I lovingly pushed her away, keeping my hands on her shoulders.

"Thank you Beloved, I can heal myself the rest of the way. If you could just assist me to that shady tree…"

"Yes," she spoke as she looked into my eyes.

Between her support and the stick I had found, I was able to hobble over to the tree and sit down on the earth between two large roots. Mytria kissed me on the forehead and ran up to get her pack.

"I will have to set this leg before I dress it," she said apologetically.

"I am ready," I replied.

Before I knew it the leg was set, my wound was cleaned and wrapped in herbs which where held in place with tree bark. Mytria washed off the sticks I had used to brace my leg, replaced them on top of the tree bark and wrapped clean cloth around them to keep them steady.

"When we get back to our camp, I can make you a proper cast," she said as she gently patted my leg.

We decided to stay there for the remainder of the day and take off for OUR home at sunrise the next day. It was an excellent decision, for that night under the stars was beyond words. Somehow we managed to make love. In fact, we made love again and again, each time going deeper and deeper into each other's very Soul, in fact, into our joint Soul.

Mytria had heard of Divine Complements during her Temple studies, and told me all she knew. And then, we had to make love again, which is when it happened. Mytria tried to keep it from me, but I knew we made a child then. How could we not? The heavens almost opened and sent her down. Yes, it would be a daughter, our daughter, our love child.

When morning came, I felt almost healed. That is, until I tried to walk.

A New Home

Doing the Work
PART III

Change

GREETINGS:

We are Mytria of the Violet Temple of Alcyone and Mytre of the Ashtar Command. We have returned to share more of our story of Pleiadian Ascension. We have decided to share this experience of our ascension with our Earth friends, as you are also entering your time of ascension. Hence, as you return to your Multidimensional SELF you will soon meet your Divine Complement, if you have not already. The term Divine Complement is also known as Twin Flame.

The more you return to your fifth dimensional resonance, the less you will feel comfortable in a body of gender. In fact, all forms of polarity will become too constrictive, too low of a resonance for your ever-expanding consciousness. Therefore, a certain urge may well rise up in you that there is someone that you must meet. You likely do not know who this person is, but you will instantly *know* your Complement when your eyes first meet. This experience is similar to catching a glimpse at yourself in a mirror.

When you contact your Complement, a chain of events will be initiated over which your ego self will have no control. The mere magnetism of meeting your own Soul in another person's body can be quite disturbing. If you are not ready for this reunion, you might even push it away. In this case, you may meet at a later time or in another reality.

On the other hand, those who are resonating to the threshold of the fifth dimension will be ready. Consequently, they will willingly change their lives in any way necessary in order to keep this person in their life. However, do not make the mistake that these intense emotions will make for an easy relationship. In fact, a relationship with your Divine Complement is much like a relationship with your self.

Your Divine Complement is the part of your Soul that you had to release to be able to inhabit a third-dimensional body of gender. After that first separation, you each took on myriad other incarnations in both male and female forms. The power of connecting with your Divine Complement is so intense, that Souls usually only choose to make this connection if they are approaching ascension. On the other hand, you could choose to ascend first and wait on the fifth dimensional threshold until your Divine Complement also ascends.

Very often, your Divine Complement over-lights you throughout your life, but you will only realize this fact after you have regained your multidimensional consciousness. Connecting with your Complement serves as the precursor to connecting with your higher expressions of SELF in the mid-fifth dimension and beyond. There are times when Divine Complements meet while both are in the physical plane. Some times they live lives of deep commitment to each other. Other times they come into Oneness to perform a great social contribution.

On the other hand, sometimes they cannot find peace together, as the energy is too intense for their state of consciousness to accept. In this case, they eventually part. The life challenge is considered a "pilot test" in which both of them realize that they are not ready to leave the third dimension. However, there was a moment of connection, which they will continue to always carry in their hearts.

In contrast, there are also lives in which you meet, merge and become ONE within your heart and Soul. However, you are forced to be apart for the sake of a Mission that is even more important than your personal love story. This final example was the case with us. But we are getting ahead of ourselves. Thus, we return to our story not too long after we left off…

MYTRIA SPEAKS:

With Mytre's injured leg, it took us several days to get back to our home base. Once there, our lives returned to normal, only at a much deeper level, as we had both completed transformative initiations. Because we had connected with our Higher Expressions, as well as with our Mother Planet, our connection to each other was even more intimate.

We shared dreams, communicated without talking, found ourselves doing similar things, as well as simultaneously thinking similar thoughts. In other words, we were experiencing a deep commitment and unconditional love for each other. That does not mean that we never argued or had difficult moments. Of course we did. However, those moments were soon over, to be replaced by our usual peace and comfort. Besides, we had something very special to share.

While Mytre's leg was healing, my stomach was growing. Our dear child was growing within my body, as well as within Mytre's heart. He often held my stomach and talked to his daughter, he insisted the baby was a girl. When we shared those moments, I was so happy that I thought my heart might burst. However, this happiness was always followed by a moment of dread.

I tried to ignore that feeling, but I knew that there would be change soon and not just the change of having our baby. The Mother was telling me that she would soon need our assistance. There were some things that She needed us to do for Her. She too was ready to expand into Her higher expression of SELF. Unfortunately, the day finally came in which all my feelings were validated.

I was very close to birthing and Mytre's leg was almost totally healed. It was early in the morning and Mytre had been taking an early morning swim at the nearby lake. I was making our morning meal, when I felt a sharp pain in my stomach. Just a few moments later, Mytre came running towards me as fast as he could, which was very fast.

I ran, wobbled towards him, but he waved for me to stop. When he reached me, he was out of breath but managed to say, "What just happened to you? We have to go back to the Village. It is your time soon and you need to be where they can help you."

I resisted his advice for days. I wanted to have my baby in the home that I loved. However, I knew Mytre was right, I just didn't know why. After I had several of these pains, he convinced me that we needed to go to the Temple. We cleaned up our camp, but left it habitable, as we planned to return as soon as it was safe for the baby. Unfortunately, life had another idea.

Birth

MYTRE SPEAKS:

I was very happy when Mytria agreed to return to the Village and to have our baby at the Temple. Since my "Vision Quest" I had been having more visions than I could peacefully contain. I knew that we had to return to the Village for the baby, but I also knew that we had to return to the Village because something there was very wrong. I made a flat cart for our "supplies," but knew that it would be for Mytria. If she walked too long, she would have the pains again, so I made her ride on the cart that I pulled.

She was not happy with my carrying all our packs and pulling the cart. However, when I reminded her that she was carrying the precious cargo of our daughter, she ceased her complaints. When we reached the hill above our village, we saw that my worst fears were correct. The force field around the village was up, which could only mean that our position had been discovered, and we were under attack. I realized then that I would not be around for the birth of our child, as I would be too busy protecting her home.

Mytria and I looked at each other with great remorse. No words were necessary. We both recognized that we would be apart and that the return to our wonderful home would be postponed indefinitely. Mytria was determined to walk into the Village, and I agreed. I wanted to feel her by my side, as I did not know when I would find her there again. Just before we entered the Force Field, Mytria, the baby and I embraced for a long moment. Our hearts and minds became ONE, as we vowed that the three of us would always be together in our consciousness.

Once I entered the code for the Force Field, and we walked through, we knew that our lives would be forever altered. The Village was in complete chaos with people running around in a somewhat organized fashion. The fear in the air was tangible. Before we could take in the situation at hand, Mytria's labor pains began and my Commanding Officer appeared from nowhere.

"Mytre, where have you been? We could not contact you, and we need you to pilot a Mission NOW!"

"I must take my mate to the Temple, she is in labor with our child."

"No! You must come now," he said as he directed one of the Protectors to take Mytria to the Temple.

"Go, my love," Mytria said bravely, with tears in her eyes. "We will be fine. Our daughter is coming now."

My Commanding Officer literally pulled me by the arm, as Mytria sat on the cart and was taken to the Temple. What was left of our life together lay forgotten on the ground. We would have only our final embrace to remind us of what we had experienced together.

MYTRIA SPEAKS:

Of course, both Mytre and I knew that something terrible was happening in the Village, but we chose not to talk about it. I had even wondered if my pains had been a warning of some kind. I thought that they were labor pains, but wondered if they were a message from our daughter. Both Mytre and I knew that she would be very special, as we often visited her together in our dreams. She told us that she was coming to prepare our people for an auspicious event.

We knew that she was correct, as we always saw the Elohim Alcyone with her in our dreams. I did not know if we, my daughter and I, would ever see Mytre again. He was a warrior, and he was going into battle. I knew that. In fact, I had known that fact almost as soon as we returned to our home after his Vision Quest. I pushed it from my mind a thousand times, but it always returned to remind me to cherish every moment of our NOW. I talked to the Mother many times, selfishly begging that our lives could remain the way they were.

She always said, "Courage my ONE. You are to be a Priestess and your daughter has a great destiny." That is all She would say. I would call again and again, until I finally tired of my weakness and accepted that The Mother was right. It was then that I began to live in the flow of the NOW. I did not understand exactly what would happen, but I knew that it would happen soon.

Hence, I determined to Unconditionally LOVE every moment that we shared. Once I surrendered into that decision, I realized that I had wasted precious time in worrying and determined to give thanksgiving for every moment that we shared from then on. But then the pains began, and I knew that our daughter was telling me that, soon, she would be born.

As we reached the stairs to the Temple, I rose from the cart. I would walk up the stairs with my head held high. Jador, the Protector, kindly supported me. As soon as he touched me I knew he was one of those whom I had met within the Core of the Mother. We would all be joining together now, for what purpose I was not sure. As we entered the door to the Temple, I saw another member of our group. Her name was Sirena. She and Jador were to be my closest friends during our impending transformation.

"We have been waiting for you. Alycia, your daughter, told us she was ready to be born." Neither one of us questioned that information. I instantly trusted Sirena and surrendered myself to her care. She swept me into the waiting birthing room. It was beautifully prepared with violet cloth draped across the walls. There candles, incense and soft music. Most important, the room was filled with love.

"We have prepared this room to the specifications of Alycia. She was very specific. All of us here feel honored to be among the ones who assist with her birth." Sirena said no more.

She led me to my birthing chair and began to cleanse my body with a mixture of herbs and clear water. She brushed my hair and pulled it back from my face, then removed my old clothing and wrapped me with a cloth as light as air. This procedure instantly put me into a deep trance in which I had the most amazing experience, which I will try to explain.

As I fell into a deep trance, I found myself again in the Core of the Mother. In front of me was Elohim Alcyone.

"I have created a form so that I can better participate in the ascension of your people," She spoke directly into my heart.

"Because you and Mytre, who are Divine Complements, were able to both pass your Initiations, your combined frequencies were high enough for me to implant the seed of my form within your body. Of course, Mytre was vital to this implantation. It was the deep, abiding love embedded in his fluid that allowed that seed to germinate. Furthermore, because the two of you had so bonded with my land, I was able to protect the growing one within your body. Now, I am here again to assist you with the birthing."

All that I can remember is that I felt a slow,

gradual release of that which I had tenaciously protected throughout my entire pregnancy. Being surrounded by the color violet, in both my inner and outer vision, created a deep calm; and the sounds, smells and flickering candles allowed me to remain in complete surrender. Suddenly, the release was complete. My journey would continue, but this time with Alycia.

Together as one essence, Alycia met Mytre, and the three of us soared into a reality in which there was total peace, unconditional love and multidimensional light. As we previewed this world, we realized that it was very familiar. Yes, it was the very world that we were now fighting to maintain. However, there was no fighting here, no fear, no war, and no separation. We all had a Core Essence, but it visibly flowed into the Core Essence of everyone and everything. In fact, there were no "things," as every form carried its own life-spark and frequency signature.

As the three of us, joined into one tight unit, floated through this world, we realized that we were in a possible reality. We also remembered that we had vowed to ground this reality into the body of our new planetary home. In fact, all of us who had met within the Core of the Mother had made this vow before we were born. Now, we were being called upon to remember all that we had vowed to do.

Mytre and I realized that our Missions would separate our forms, but never our hearts. I was to protect and assist in raising Alycia, who would also be raised by the Priests and Priestesses of our Temple. Time would be moving very quickly now, and Mother Alcyone would need our assistance, as we would need Hers. My beloved Mytre may or may not return in the form in which I had known him. However, soon we would no longer be limited to these forms, so any loss would be temporary. I tried to remember that fact during the long dark nights of my empty bed.

Fortunately, I returned from my vision to find Alycia in my arms.

How can I describe the agony of loosing my Divine Complement and the ecstasy of birthing the child of our great love within the same day? Fortunately, it was the intense oppositions of these two emotions of deepest grief and abounding joy that forced me to find a place to live in-between these two extremes.

With my every breath, I held Mytre within my heart and protected him with my every thought. Many of our communication systems were down or restricted. Therefore, I was not able hear any word of him for what would be measured by you in years.

It was only our meetings in our dream world and the bliss of raising Alycia that kept me going. I knew that Mytre's contribution to the ascension of our people, as well as the reality in which we lived, was great. I was extremely proud of him, but I still constantly missed him. Actually, I missed US!

Mind Over Matter

MYTRE SPEAKS:

When I had to choose between my family and my duty, the answer was simple. I chose my family. However, Mytria urged me to go, to do my duty, to help make our world safe for our daughter. In the moment that I paused, making my decision, I was swept away and so was my family. I was desolate. How could I have let that happen? Why had I made her come back to the Village? Why didn't I pull away from my Commander and run towards my family?

These questions haunted me and destroyed my ability to concentrate. I sat in on important missions and could not focus. I had nothing to give to the Protectors, to my family or to myself. Yes, myself, I had to find my Self. However, there was no time to do that. We were under attack. Our long-range communications were down, many of our Ships had been destroyed before they even left the atmosphere and the Force Field around the village was weakening more each day.

We needed reinforcements. We needed the Arcturians to come to our assistance. We still had our fastest Scout Ship, and I was one of our best pilots. Before I had a chance to think, I stood up and volunteered. It was as if someone else made that decision, but once said, I had to follow through. A moment before that decision I was concerned about my loved ones, and now I was likely going to my death. What was I thinking? Actually, *who* was thinking? It was not my conflicted ego. Therefore, I hoped it was the ME that I had met on my Vision Quest.

I suppose that is was that version of me that activated my decision, because as soon as it was made, everything changed. Before I knew it, three others and I were flying our Ship through the small area of unguarded space we had found. We made it through only to be greeted by a War Ship. Somehow we evaded them long enough for one of our Ships to take down the War Ship. However, we were dead in space. All our controls were out, and life-support was minimal.

Our battle had diminished our crew from four to three. We were safe for a while, but would likely be found by an enemy Ship at any moment. What could I do? It was then that I became the ME who I had seen on my Vision Quest. If I could talk to rocks, dirt, sky and the Mother, why couldn't I also talk to the Ship? Our Ships all had implanted biological elements. Maybe I could connect with whatever life force remained in those jell packs.

I felt the adrenaline racing through my body and knew that I had to find my Core. I thought of my first meeting with Mytria in the Core of Alcyone and used that memory to find my own Core. In fact,

I finally remembered the message I was given by the Arcturian. It had said, as it looked into my Soul, "YOU can do it!" I still had no idea what that meant.

However, suddenly, I was floating with Mytria and our newborn daughter through a potential reality of complete safety, total love and absolute unity. I felt my essence intermingle with every person, plant, animal and thing within this world. I heard a part of me saying, "Stop day dreaming and get back to business," but another part of me—the floating part of me — was saying, "Pay attention to this message."

Yes, this vision, or reality, was a message. I was being shown how to merge with all life, just as I had done when I found my way off the cliff. Therefore, instead of judging my vision/experience, I totally surrendered to it. I merged with each person I met in this reality. I merged with every plant, every animal, and finally, with every "thing." It was when I totally merged with what appeared to me to be a rock, that I heard the Ship's engines come online.

Outside my inner image I heard my crewmates yelling at me to open my eyes and help them. However, I chose to attend to the loving support of my family who was assisting me to merge with every component of this potential reality. I let go of every external perception and directed all my attention into the movement of this "rock." Slowly, the rock lifted up off the ground and began to move through the air. Simultaneously, our Ship slowly began to move.

I stayed within my inner reality, as I knew that the others could steer the Ship. It was up to me make it move. The rock in my image hovered before me, as if awaiting instructions. I focused all my attention on the closest Arcturian Starship and directed those coordinates into the rock in my image. Slowly the rock turned and began to move. My eyes were closed, and I dared not open them. I had to trust that the Ship was moving in the correct direction.

I then saw many other rocks moving towards my rock, and I assumed that our enemy had found us. I could not be distracted by a battle, so I made my rock invisible to the other rocks and directed it to move beyond the speed of light. Instantly, my rock was free of the other rocks. The rock was moving faster than I could track. If I lost sight of it in my image, how could I control it?

"Let go!" I heard an inner voice say. I didn't know what I was supposed to let go of, so I let go of everything and passed out. I woke up as the two crewmembers lifted me up and put me into the Captains Chair.

"You did it," they said in one voice.

"What did I do," I said, still wondering if my entire experience had been my imagination.

"You piloted the Ship with your mind!"

All I could say was, "Can you take over from here? I think I am going to pass out again."

In the distance, I heard, "Yes Sir," as I returned

to my vision. This time my focus was on my family and on the Elohim Alcyone who was with them. It was She who spoke to me.

"Our dear Mytre, we are most pleased with your ability to remember your innate ability. Do you remember how you first learned that facility in the sixth dimension of Arcturus?"

"Yes, I think so," I replied. "But I thought I was a Pleiadian?"

"Our dear Ascending ONE, you are many beings within ONE. You have chosen to take a form among these brave people. They were tired of fighting and sought to live in peace and love so that they could return to their higher frequencies of SELF.

"The only way to assure that these Ones can remain safe is if they ascend their bodies, and their entire reality, into the fifth dimension. In this way, they will live beyond the perception of their enemies. You, Mytria and your daughter Alycia have dedicated yourselves to this transition. In fact, everyone who you met within the Core of the Mother has dedicated themselves to this process of ascension."

As the great Elohim spoke, myriad memories, images, thoughts and emotions filled my consciousness, and surprisingly, I was able to understand them all simultaneously.

"Did I really move the Ship?" I had to ask.

"We, that is the energy of the ONE, moved the Ship."

I understood that. When I was in this reality of the ONE, I could be the catalyst for anything. It was the great love of my family that brought me to this reality, and it was my great love for them that gave me the courage to release any glimpse of fear from my consciousness.

"You are correct," the Elohim said in response to my thoughts. "Yes, we heard your thoughts even before they were expressed as words. Your thoughts, as you have found, have great power. That is why you had to pass your Initiation. Only unconditional love could hold you within that frequency of reality. Furthermore, those with negative intentions cannot even perceive, much less enter or harm, that world."

With the assurance of those final words, I returned to the reality of my Ship. I was instantly greeted by the joyous vision of the Arcturian Starship. I was to study onboard that Starship for many years to learn how to adapt all our Starships to travel by the power of thought.

The most difficult part of that assignment was that no one could know of my secret mission. Fortunately, I could meet with Mytria and Alycia in our fifth dimensional reality, but that was the only contact we could have. The Arcturians sent reinforcements to assist our Village and the surrounding areas. Nevertheless, we all knew that expanding the resonance of our society into the fifth dimension was our only hope for long-term peace

Suzanne Lie

Here and Now

MYTRIA SPEAKS:

When I was separated from Mytre in the chaotic moment of our return to our Village, I was temporally brave. I had to release him to his Higher Mission, give birth to our daughter and accept the process of being a new mother—alone—all in the same fateful day. I also had to accept the fact that I would have to live each day without Mytre, my Divine Complement.

Fortunately, the three of us, Mytre, our daughter Alycia and I, met every night in our Astral Bodies. However, an "astral hug" is not the same as a physical embrace. At first the nightly visits were enough, but eventually they only added to the pain of missing Mytre. These nightly meetings were the only contact that Alycia had ever had with her father, so it was normal to her. On the other hand, sometimes it made me miss Mytre more.

After many years of these meetings, I began to let Alycia go alone, using the excuse that I had to get a deep sleep that night. Gradually, I joined Mytre and Alycia less and less. I had to create my own life. I could no longer hold on to something that was not a part of my physical reality.

I don't know when it was that I decided that I would see him one more time, and then I would have to end our nightly meetings. But, eventually, that night came. Of course, Alycia knew that it was a good night for her to NOT join us, as she always knew what was in my mind. In fact, she could read the mind, heart and aura of everyone, all the time.

When I showed up to meet Mytre without Alycia, he instantly knew why. "I can no longer pretend that this is enough for me." I said before I lost my nerve. "I will wait for you forever, but I have to find my SELF again. When I bonded with you so deeply, then gave birth to our child, I seemed to have lost a part of myself. My meditations have been about how to wait for you. Everything I do has been with you in mind. I deny myself deep friendships, as I can only think of you..."

For a very brief moment, I felt his physical arms around me, but all I could do was sob. I wanted more! This was not enough! I had to find something inside of my SELF that was as important as being with him.

The feeling of his arms around me disappeared. He looked into my eyes and said in a disappointed way, "I have been working for years to manifest my form with you, but I have waited too long. I have lost you."

"No, no," I cried. "You have not lost me. You will never lose me. The problem is that I have lost my SELF."

"I understand," is all that he said, as his astral body disappeared from my vision. I knew that he did not want to show me how much I had hurt him.

I knew that he understood, but I was still angry and hurt. "Good" I thought. "I can use this anger to release him."

Alycia still met with Mytre every night, but told me nothing about their meetings. I was very happy about their meetings. She deserved to have personal time with her father, and he deserved to watch her change and grow. In fact, Alycia was growing much quicker than was normal. It had been only about twelve years, but she was almost an adult. I knew that this was because she was also the manifest form of the Elohim of Alcyone.

I was sad that Alycia did not need me in the same way, but I also knew that it was time for me to stop hiding from my own power. I remembered how, long ago, I had been able to connect with the Mother in a deep and intimate manner. However, I seemed to have lost that power when I became a mother myself. What was I to do? Who was I to be?

I was thinking about that fated day of our return to our Village when I lost Mytre, Alycia was born and I lost my SELF. Could I somehow retrace that day? Where and when did I loose my deep connection with the Mother? It was then that I heard the Inner Voice for the first time since that day.

"You will find your answer within my womb," I heard the Mother say. But then Her voice was silent. My first message was to find the Mother's Womb.

For days I went through all my duties repeating, "The Womb of the Mother. Where is the womb of the Mother?" Then, one morning I awoke with the answer. The Womb of the Mother was the Sacred Rock that I had somehow entered the day I met the Mother in the form of the Elohim Alcyone. I had to return there. I had to return, right now.

Again, I packed a light pack and snuck out into the early dawn. Only this time, I first informed Alycia, who completely understood why I had to go. It had been many years since Mytre and I had left our cave by the Sacred Rock. There had been many changes to our Village and our way of life since then. We all knew that the Arcturians had given us temporary protection from our enemies. However, we also knew that we would have to actively participate in the ascension of which they had spoken.

Living all these years in the Violet Temple had protected me from the fear and confusion that was far too common in the Village. However, my people needed some answers, and these answers could only come from the Mother. I walked for two and a half days before I found the Sacred Rock. Changes had been made to the nearby landscape, but the unseen energy shield, which could only be entered by the "invited one," protected the Sacred Rock and its surrounding area.

I felt a floating sensation when I moved through the shield. Then, I had to move through many bushes before I could find the exact location on the rock that had once taken me into the Mother's Womb. Once I found the Rock, I surveyed the area.

It looked deserted and unkempt. Therefore, I spent the greater part of what was left of the day cleaning out my nearby cave and setting up my temporary home. This time I knew just what I needed to bring, so the work went quickly.

When the cave was fully repaired and made into a cozy home, I stood back to observe it. It was then that I fell to the floor sobbing. Every memory of my time here with Mytre overtook me, and I was overwhelmed with sorrow. I had not allowed myself to feel this sorrow since I had sent him away, and it felt good to finally release it. When I could cry no more, I crawled over to what had been our sleeping place, pulled myself into a fetal position and slept like an infant.

I awoke a new person, clear headed and determined to fulfill my destiny. I went out to the small pond that was still there, but a bit overgrown. Then, without thought, I spent most of the morning pulling out plants that had invaded the pond and clearing out the moss that settled between these plants.

I re-created my rock fire pit, moved some limbs and rocks to make seating around the fire and cleared the area of unwanted rocks and plants. I even dug up the area that had once been my small garden, and planted the seeds I had brought with me. Now it was time to clear a pathway to the Sacred Rock and pull away unwanted plants from the Portal into the Mother's Womb.

I had come to realize that the Sacred Rock was a

powerful Portal, but I had told no one about it, even my best friends in the Temple. My first initiation had been when I was guided to this area. My second initiation, which was NOW, was to protect this Sacred Space. With that thought in mind, I suddenly remembered what the Arcturian had whispered into my Soul that first night in the Mother's Womb. "You are a Keeper of the Violet Fire."

I had forgotten that message because I did not know what the Violet Fire was. However, most of my lessons in the Temple had been about the power of transmutation that was contained within the Violet Fire. We often spoke of the "myth" of this Fire, but no one knew what or where it was, even myself. I had been so distracted by missing Mytre that much of what I had learned went into my unconscious mind.

Now that I was back on the Land of the Mother, all the pieces of the puzzle were falling together. However, I only knew what I was supposed to do in the NOW. Once done, I again knew what to do in that NOW. I was similar to one of the many rocks that I had moved. I was only right NOW and right HERE. I found that experience to be wonderful.

I could not remember the past and the future was NOW. I had forgotten what had happened before except for Mytre, Alycia and my dearest friends, and I had no sense of the future. Only love could guide my thoughts and my only emotion was clarity. I had never thought of clarity as an emotion, but I discovered that it was the only emotion left when I was completely focused on the HERE and NOW.

The Perception of Perception

MYTRIA CONTINUES:

Once I settled into living in the NOW, my consciousness began to completely alter. I was aware that I had not attempted to enter the Portal on the Sacred Rock, but I had no concerns about that. I knew that when it was the NOW to open the portal, I would do so without forethought. I was aware that I was in the process of expanding my resonance. When I entered the Portal before, it was opened for me, and I literally fell through it. I knew instinctively that to open the Portal myself would be a different matter.

As my consciousness expanded, I became increasingly aware of the Land and of my own Spirit. As I became more aware of my own Spirit, I began to *feel* the Spirit of the Land. Then, before I knew it, I was in Unity Consciousness with every rock, plant, tree, animal, bird, the sky and the weather. When I awoke I knew exactly what to wear and exactly which tasks would best suit the weather.

Our weather had become quite erratic in the last ten years since we knew it was time for us to ascend. Now that I was becoming ONE with the land and sky, I could understand why. As I became more and more connected with my environment, I could see how my every thought and emotion influenced it. For example, one day I awoke to see a clear sky. For some unknown reason I thought, "Oh how lovely. I hope it doesn't rain today."

Instantly, the sky began to cloud up. To make sure that I did not create the clouds I said, in a very loving way, "Thank you for your beautiful clear sky." Instantly, the clouds disappeared and the entire day was sunny and clear. I was only one person, but I had expanded my consciousness to hold the power of many. Then, I understood why the weather around the Village had become so erratic.

Many of the people there were happy and excited about the possibility of their ascension. However, at the same time they were frightened that they would not be *able* to ascend. This collective uncertainty about their fate gave the Weather Deva and her myriad Elementals many confusing messages. I had learned in the Temple that they are fourth dimensional sentient beings that serve to manifest the thoughts and emotions of Planetary Keepers.

In our case, the Planetary Keepers were humanoid, but in other worlds the Planetary Keepers were of other species. However, the energy field, which is comprised of the Keepers' thoughts and feelings, directed the Elementals and their Higher Expressions of Devas, to manifest the Keepers' needs.

A New Home

I had learned from my time on the Land that in order to ascend into the fourth and/or fifth dimensions, we would need to learn mastery of our energy field. Our people had lived in strife and battle for so long that it was difficult for them to release the sense of victimization and the lack of power that came with that state of mind. I know that I had struggled greatly with my feelings of being a victim to the loss of my beloved Mytre.

Fortunately, now that I had returned to the Mother, I was beginning to understand exactly why our separation needed to occur. We had to be apart in order to be fully focused on the transmutation of our consciousness. But, I had to wait until Alycia was old enough to be cared for by our friends in the Temple before I too, could go off on my own.

I realized that there were many women in the Village who could not leave their children and go off into the wilderness as I had. However, each of us had different destinies, and some of these men and women had the destiny of guiding and protecting the children. Furthermore, the children who had been born since our Ascension Process had begun were often much more evolved than their parents. This was the case with Alycia.

With only myself to think of and care for, I was able to greatly escalate the expansion of my consciousness. It was when I realized how my energy field affected the weather that I knew I was ready to open the Portal. However, I would patiently wait (I was finally learning patience) until the NOW in which I found myself standing before the Sacred Rock.

In the meantime, I went about my daily life, monitoring my every thought and emotion in order to remain in the NOW of the ONE and in Unity with All Life. During each passing day, I came to more fully understand why everything that had happened to me was a component of the fulfillment of my Mission. I remembered the connection that I had with the Mother before I had become a Mother myself and understood how I could more deeply merge with the Great Mother now that I had a child.

I could also see how being a Father had assisted Mytre in the same manner. I was beginning to realize that ALL is Perfect within the ONE. It is only the fearful reactions of our lower nature that denied us the perception of perfection.

As my consciousness expanded, the Sacred Rock began to call me. Living in the NOW had taught me that patience was the key to balancing my energy field. Whenever I fell into a desire, I was pulled out of the NOW and into a "time" in which I was lacking and needed more. While in the NOW, there was no lack, for I was in the Flow of Divine Manifestation of my every need.

In fact, many of these manifestations occurred even before my brain was aware they were necessary. With this realization, I became aware of my Spirit Essence which is an expression of my SELF in a higher frequency of reality. A "higher frequency of reality" was a new concept to me. In the Temple we learned about Spirit Guides and Angels, but no one had considered that these Beings could be higher expressions of our humanoid form.

At first, it was quite difficult for me to break away from the traditions in which I had been raised and the spiritual teachings I had learned. However, while in the NOW, all doubt was impossible. In other words, at the second that I allowed doubt to enter my consciousness, I fell out of the NOW and into my mundane consciousness. This experience was like falling from a high, warm cliff into a cold, muggy pond.

After the first few "fallouts," actually it took many; I began to realize that doubt was the reason for my immediate decline into an old way of life. When I had the fallouts, I usually felt angry, depressed and anxious for days or even weeks. Then, gradually, I learned to forgive myself for my distrust of Spirit, which was actually the higher expression of my SELF.

Eventually, I realized that most of my habit of doubting occurred because I was afraid that my happiness was "too good to be true." That habit came from the remnants of my being a victim. After all, a victim is a martyr who can never be healed. I had already spent too many years of my life suffering in that manner and was ready to change my mind in order to change my habits.

As I remembered to forgive myself for falling out of my expanded consciousness, I could remain in that state of mind much longer. Now it was fatigue that caused me to fall out of my higher consciousness. Therefore, I learned to keep track of the needs of my physical body. Did I need to feed it? Did it need to rest? I discovered that if I was hungry or tired that it was far more difficult to be the Master of my energy.

Finally, the day came when I knew it was the NOW to open the Portal.

Opening The Portal

MYRTIA CONTINUES:

The morning after I felt it was the NOW to open the Portal I awoke just before dawn. I had not planned to awaken at that time, so it must have been my Spirit who made that decision. Instantly, I knew it was to be a sacred day. Therefore, after washing, dressing and drinking some water, I went to my special rock just above my campsite to watch the rising Sun.

As soon as I climbed onto the rock, I fell into a deep meditation. Even when I felt the warmth of the Sun's first rays on my face, I kept my eyes closed. Then, with my physical eyes closed I saw the Sunrise with my Third Eye. What a glorious vision that was!

Through my Third Eye, I was able to perceive colors that were invisible to my physical vision. Also, I could feel the higher frequency of these rays just above my heart. I remembered an ancient "myth" that we studied in the Temple about the existence of a High Heart just above our physical heart.

Did looking at the sunrise through my Third Eye open my High Heart? I could not ponder that question long, for instantly my body began trembling so vigorously that I almost fell off the rock. I felt the energy originate from the base of my own womb and rise up my spine. The energy was hot, then cold, then hot again.

I was shaking so much that I could hardly stay conscious when I heard, "Pull the energy into your Core!" I was not sure how to do that, so I imagined that I could breathe the energy into my Core. Gradually the energy calmed, like water that had found a place on the land that could encompass its flow.

Now my body began to undulate to the flow of the energy, which appeared to be directed by my breath. I slowed my breathing to calm my mind, taking long slow inhales and exhaling twice as long as my inhales.

It was then that I felt the River of LIFE flowing through my Core. However, this was not a river of water. It was a river of light. As the light of the Sun rose higher in the sky, the top of my head began to glow and pulse.

I could feel the sunlight entering the top of my head and felt the light from above interacting with the Flow of light from the base of my spine. From the top of my head to my High Heart I could feel the two sources of light interact and intermingle.

I was observing the inside of my form as if I was looking through a Portal. Yes, the first Portal I had to open was the Portal to my SELF, my own Core.

I sat there the entire day, without drinking or

eating and barely moving. I don't know how I did it. In fact, I have not been able to do it since. However, on that fated day, I was able to completely surrender. I am not sure what I surrendered to, but it changed my life forever. Perhaps, I surrendered to my Destiny.

As the sun began to set, I could feel that its great light had traveled all the way down into the base of my spine. As the sun totally set, I fell back onto the rock and slept until the next dawn.

Again, I awoke just before dawn, but this time I was very hungry. However, I was not sure I would be able to walk, much less climb off of the rock, so I laid there until there was adequate light. I stretched my body and tried to remember what had happened the day before. The last thing I could remember was climbing onto the rock and beginning to meditate. Then, my mind went blank.

"It will come to you, as you are ready to use it." I heard the now familiar inner voice. I had learned to trust that voice completely. Therefore, I sat up, slowly stood and carefully crawled down off the rock.

When I got to my campsite I fell into the pool, clothes and all, and stayed there for hours. Finally, hunger forced me out of my water womb, for indeed I had been reborn. Climbing out of the pond and trying to stand and walk made me feel like an infant. It was as if someone else was in charge of my body. However, that someone else felt so kind, loving and patient, that it was just fine.

When I went to eat, I realized the first way in which I had changed. I could not find anything that my body would accept as food, except for water. Therefore, I drank lots and lots of water. Finally, I found some herbs that I had dried, and I made them into tea. My new body accepted the tea, as well. I was beginning to understand just how important and complete this re-birth process had been.

Within the next few days I found some nutrients that my body would accept. All of them had to be from the land such as certain grasses and flowers. I had to trust my instincts to make sure that I wasn't eating something poisonous. Fortunately, my updated form was completely integrated with the land and knew what to eat and what not to eat.

I lost all sense of time and I was awake during the day or the night for many hours, or for only a few. There was no one to care for and nothing to do. Hence, I could completely embrace my process and follow my every inner direction at the exact NOW in which I received it.

I knew that my body was changing in resonance because I could perceive things that I could never perceive before, such as the auras around each plant. It was the aura of the plants that told me whether or not to eat it. If the aura was blue to violet, it was fine for me to eat. However, if the aura was green to red, I could not. I enjoyed this new skill of seeing the resonance of all life and walked around my camp observing all the auras.

Eventually, I wandered beyond the confines of

my camp and found myself at the Lake where I had met Mytre. I had been avoiding the lake, as it made me feel too sad to be there. However, now the lake brought me joy, and I spent the greater part of the day swimming and resting by the water. As the sun lowered on the horizon, I knew it was time to return.

I was walking over the same ledge that I had walked over the evening I met Mytre when I saw a figure standing there. He looked much like Mytre, but I knew that was impossible. Nonetheless, I ran to the where the figure stood, to be suddenly embraced by the strong arms of my beloved.

I began to sob for joy, as I felt his physical arms around me. We stood together as one being for what seemed like forever, until I heard him say, "I am not really here now. This is my Astral Projection." I pushed away from him in disappointment and anger.

"But you feel so real. How can that be?"

"Do not be angry, my love, we made this agreement during your awakening."

I could not remember any agreement, but I never knew him to lie to me.

"Oh Mytre, you have become so powerful. I am so very proud of you, my love. How long can you stay like this?"

Mytre smiled and said, "I do not know, but I have been instructed to take you to the Sacred Rock by midnight."

"Did the Mother call you too?" I asked.

"You have called me, which is why I have learned this skill of teleportation. It was my deep need to hold you in my arms that forced me to open the latent DNA that held this innate ability."

"Yes," I said, "And I would never had made this journey if you were not away from me. That which we saw as a disaster was actually our destiny."

We walked arm in arm to the Sacred Rock and stood before it as the last rays of the Sun dropped below the horizon. We had several hours before midnight, so we sat arm-in-arm and told each other everything that had happened to us since we had parted. The time we spent together felt like an eternity, yet it was also far too short.

When it was almost midnight, Mytre's image began to fade in and out. We knew that our time together was almost over. He had come to assist me in opening the Portal, my initiation, and I had been his initiation to teleport so far away and for such a long time.

When it was almost midnight, we held each other very closely. His form began to flicker in and out, as if he was loosing a connection. In fact, he said that he was loosing the connection with his physical form and would have to leave now or greatly harm his body. I released him with a final kiss, turned away from him and faced the Sacred Rock.

I knew that he had left, but our heart connection had been strengthened. I could feel it in my High Heart. He had given me the courage and confidence that I needed to open the Portal. With my mind at peace and my heart filled with love, I bent forward and touched the Sacred Rock with the palm of my right hand.

Instantly, I felt my connection with the Portal. Keeping my hand on the Rock, I moved closer and closer until I was standing just inches from its surface. I slowly dropped my hand and inched forward until my toes were touching the Rock. Then I leaned forward until my heart was touching the Rock.

I heard a whirling noise and felt a light breeze that appeared to come from the Rock. I waited as the breeze became a wind and the wind became a torrent. The sound was so loud that it almost hurt my ears, but I did not move.

I closed my eyes to better see through my Third Eye and discovered a light coming from the center of the Rock. I touched this light and felt my hand move into the Rock. With my hand before me I took my first step into the Rock and through the Portal. It was then that the noise became so loud that it hurt my ears and the light so bright that my Third Eye ached, but I continued my forward motion.

Suddenly, I was pulled through a swirling matrix of light and sound. I was totally disoriented and could not tell up from down. In fact, I think I was spinning around. I used all the mind control I had learned to avoid nausea and called to the Mother to pull me through this Portal and into Her Womb at the Core of our planet.

It seemed forever before the swirling stopped. Then I was almost pushed out of the vortex and landed on the cool earth in total darkness. I rose to my feet and awaited the Mother. Slowly I acclimated to the darkness and the denser atmosphere, until I could see that I was in the same cave in which I first met the Mother, Elohim Alcyone.

"Dear Mother, I have come to you," I whispered, almost to my self.

In a sudden flash of white light the Mother appeared before me with outstretched arms and a warm heart.

"Congratulations, my dear, you have opened my Portal."

A New Home

Life With the Arcturians
PART IV

Suzanne Lie

Creating Reality

MYTRE SPEAKS:

I continue my story during a time when our Pleiadian Ascension was entering the same ascension phase, as your Earth is experiencing. This phase is the process of integrating the higher frequency light into your earth vessels, emotions and neural synapses of thought and actions. This integration of higher light enables you to awaken your innate potential as the creator of your reality.

When Mytria and I spent our time together with the Mother, we were instructed to fully embrace the escalating electromagnetic fields of light that were bombarding our planet. These energies were activating synapses in our brains, which allowed us to absorb new information. Hence, Mytria was able to open the Portal into the Core of the planet, and I was able to steer the Starship with my mind.

In order to come into these initiations, we had to release ALL of our old patterns of thought and emotion. Free of these limiting patterns of thought and energy, we could surrender to the unknown and enter the chaos of immense change.

You, our ascending friends on Earth, are NOW being called upon to undergo that same process by:

• Releasing limitation

- Surrendering to the unknown
- Entering the chaos
- Acting in a novel fashion.

RELEASING LIMITATIONS

When you realize that you must *release old patterns of limitation* you are faced with the realization that YOU are the creator of your life. Since you do NOT know how you can make the best choices, you recognize that all you can do is to surrender to the chaos of extreme change.

When your patterns of limitation are broken, you are propelled into great evolutionary leaps of consciousness. Through this higher consciousness you can more easily integrate the higher light and become a Master of Energy.

When I had to leave Mytria at the very moment that our daughter was being born, my heart was broken and my mind was in total chaos. I was faced with an impossible situation. I needed to be with my wife and birthing child, but I also had to make their reality safe. Then, when our Space Craft was attacked and the controls were down, I was able to connect with an innate ability I never knew I had, in order to move and steer the Ship with my mind.

We did make it to the nearest Arcturian Starship, but just barely. Fortunately, they had picked up a signal that our wounded ship was approaching them and they came to our rescue. We were immediately taken to their Restoration Chamber. Being in this Chamber not only restored me to my former health, but it also stabilized the new neural synapses that I had activated when I moved the Ship.

My Final Initiation of bilocating myself to visit and assist Mytria during her Initiation of opening the Portal moved us both into a higher frequency of expression. From this higher frequency of expression, we can better assist you in remembering *your* innate abilities, which were forgotten during your long sojourn into the third dimension. Just as the Arcturians often told me, it is important that you know that you are NOT learning. You are REMEMBERING.

Learning can cause a fear of failure and doubt about whether or not you can learn. On the other hand, remembering, although frustrating at times, forces you to recognize your higher expressions of SELF, a great antidote for any fear. However, there are many emotions that you will need to embrace and release during your deep communications with your true SELF.

SURRENDERING TO THE UNKNOWN

The earth vessel that you are wearing was created from the third dimensional elements and the fourth dimensional Elementals that enliven your form. However, Earth is raising Her resonance. Since matching the resonance with a given reality is how you adhere to that world, you will need to match your resonance with ascending Earth to continue your personal ascension.

In other words, in order to remain attached to the Matrix of Ascending Earth, you must *surrender to the unknown* in order to stay in entrainment with the frequency of Gaia's Earth. Entrainment is the practice of matching your brainwaves to a desired frequency whereby you and other oscillating systems can interact to assume the same frequency of expression.

Therefore, when you match your energy field with the electromagnetic field of Earth, Her rise in frequency will pull you along in Her wake. In the same manner, your personal ascension energy field assists the planetary ascension. Through entrainment, the higher frequencies of light that are bombarding Earth change not only Earth but all Her inhabitants, as well.

The resonant frequency of any reality must be matched, entrained, in order for you to experience that frequency of reality. Many of you have begun your inter-dimensional explorations and are finding that fact to be true. What you may not have discovered yet is that you CAN DO ANYTHING you place your intention upon and then fill with unconditional love.

Your thoughts are your personal light synapses that entrain your thinking with the different frequencies of your mental light matrix. Furthermore, you can entrain your mental matrix with any possible realty by projecting unconditional love onto that matrix.

The unconditional love both opens the Portal

into that reality and binds you to that reality. Unfortunately, a forgotten program is an unused program. Therefore, many of your higher frequency mental programs have been forgotten. Auspiciously, it is during this phase of ascension that your multidimensional memory returns.

EMBRACING THE CHAOS

As I said at the beginning of my message, your reality is in the same phase of ascension as our reality was when I opened my mind to my innate powers. There are many extreme changes that must be made during this phase of ascension because the old, third/fourth-dimensional patterns are in juxtaposition with the incoming, fifth-dimensional energy patterns. These conflicting energy patterns create the chaos that precedes great change.

In order to entrain your energy with the fifth dimensional energy, you must release all your third dimensional thinking, emotions, habits and behaviors. If you choose to ignore what is going on around you, rather than surrendering to the chaos of radical change, you will remain entrained with the third dimension and will not become entrained with the fifth dimensional energies of ascending Earth.

When you *must* adapt in order to survive and/or stay the course of ascension, you will find the courage to enter the chaos. Happily, leaving the familiar allows you to begin the activation of long-forgotten matrixes within your brain. Fortunately, when you are faced with a new challenge, you can find the courage to enter the unknown with an open mind.

It is the open mind that is so vital. If you judge a possible shift in your thinking, you will close that door and remain stuck in patterns of thought that have become obsolete. You ascending ones are in the same situation that I was in while on the Ship. If you do not find a way to call upon your forgotten resources, you will not be able to experience the long awaited "take off" into new territories of reality.

If moving into the unknown frightens you, think how afraid you will be if you miss this moment. Fear is very illogical and can be contained by logical thinking. As soon as you speak to your fear, you are in a superior position to that emotion. This is what I had to do on the Ship when I was afraid that I could not move the Ship with my mind.

First, I had to calm my fear by telling it, "Thank you for sharing that we are in a dangerous situation. Listen to me Fear, I need you to calm down NOW so that I can take charge of this situation." Once you talk to your fear in an authoritative manner, your consciousness raises beyond the unconscious reaction of Fight/Flight and into the consciousness of mastery of your energy.

Also, if you continually monitor the thoughts that you allow to stay in your mind and the emotions that fill your body, you are already becoming the authority over the energy field that you hold in your body and project out into your world. In fact, becoming the Master of your Energy is the basis of activating your multidimensional perceptions and abilities.

ACTING IN A NOVEL FASHION

This chaos forces you to adapt by engaging in deep introspection so that you can call upon forgotten resources. Through this deep inner inspection you will re-connect with your multidimensional thinking. Your multidimensional thinking is coded to receive the Light Language of the higher frequencies of reality.

Then, via Light Language, you will receive all the assistance that you need in order to act in a novel fashion. Your first novel action will be to project your consciousness into the Core of any person, place or thing with which you are interacting. In order to project your mind into the Core of that which you wish to interact or alter, you must first go into the Core of your SELF.

It is through your own Core that you enter into the NOW. Your Multidimensional SELF lives in the NOW, and is in constant connection with your third/fourth dimensional expression serving as your anchor into Earth. TIME is your anchor to the physical plane. Time, as you know it, only exists in the third/fourth dimension. It is your attachment to time that pulls you OUT of the NOW of the ONE.

Within the NOW, you are also within the ONE. When you are ONE with all life, you can commune with every particle of reality and request that it agrees to follow your request. In other words, the effort of guiding the Ship with my mind was, primarily, the effort that it took for me to calm my fears and enter the NOW.

Once I was in the NOW, I was ONE with the multidimensional matrix of the Ship. Therefore, I could ignore the portions of the Ship that were offline and activate the fourth dimensional matrix, which was beyond any physical destruction.

Within the NOW of the ONE, which is best accessed through your own Core, you can connect with the higher frequency matrix of any manifestation to repair, activate and/or enter that matrix. Also, within the NOW you are free of time and can easily move along the time spectrum to make changes in the matrix.

In fact, entering the time matrix of Earth has often been used to correct a course of possible destruction. Unfortunately, this skill can be, and has been, misused to control and dominate. This misuse of Earth's planetary timeline matrix is a primary reason why we Galactics have been given permission to assist a free will planet.

I will return soon to discuss the process of Mind over Matter in greater depth.

Mytre of the Ashtar command

Spontaneous Awakening

MYTRE CONTINUES:

At this point in your Personal/Planetary Ascension Process, more and more of you are having Spontaneous Awakenings. These awakenings often occur after a long bout of depression, anxiety, illness or "bad luck." These awakenings occur because the multidimensional light bombarding your planet is so intense that the light quotient of humanity is rising to Critical Mass.

At this point, the majority of humans are still struggling through the third/fourth dimension. However, the light of the awakened ones is so intense that it over-shines the darkness of those who are lost in the briar patch of third dimensional turmoil. In fact, an awakened person holds ten times more light than their un-awakened companions.

The differences between the two expressions of human consciousness create chaotic energy fields because the juxtaposition between the third/fourth and fifth dimensional parallel realities is causing a paradigm shift in your world. It was the same in my world when we entered this phase of ascension.

You, the awakening ones can no longer hide in your illusions. Thus, you must enter into the chaos of the many changes that are occurring within the

NOW of your reality. It is the shift from the perceived safety of a familiar and apparently ordered world that is causing the Spontaneous Awakening.

The lies that you have been told, and the ones that you have told yourself to make life "good enough," no longer work to hide your disillusionment. The "things" you buy do not give you the same pleasure, those important people you befriended are no longer interesting, that job that gave you so much prestige has become a hollow victory, and the money you worked so hard to make is gone before you can enjoy it. "What is this all about?" you ponder.

What you may not know is that your higher expression of SELF is looking you over and waiting for this very opportunity to jar your comfortable denial. Your Multidimensional SELF gives you dreams, ideas, and opportunities for change and constantly speaks to you in the back of your mind.

"What is that nagging voice?" you ask. "My life is JUST FINE," you say, a little too loud. But as much as you push away the growing wave of transformation, the chaos of change expands more and more until you are overwhelmed. But, what are you overwhelmed with? You do not know. You cannot understand. Your life is just as it was when you thought it was great. Why are you suddenly so miserable?

It is the Light. The higher frequencies of light are erasing the third dimensional indoctrinations and replacing them with the Multidimensional Operating System. With the download of your new mental operating system, your biological computer brain can no longer compute information in the same logical, sequential manner. Many multidimensional messages are swirling through your brain and altering your neurological circuitry. These surges of high frequency light are creating sudden crashes of old mental computations.

"Am I losing my mind?" you wonder. No, you are just uploading a new mental system, and right now you are in-between the old system of computation and the new system of Flowing with the Light. The many sequential details that have filled your brain are at right angles to the circular flow of the Light Language embedded in the higher frequency light.

Some of you know that you are awakening, and some of you have been awakened for a while. It is these awakened ones who need to connect with each other and with the newly awakening ones. In this manner, the awakened ones can learn to be fifth dimensional leaders and the newly-awakening ones can gain the assistance of those who have completed the process which they have just begun.

With a core group of humanity openly saying there is a reason for what is happening, the fear of mental breakdown is replaced with a hunger for change. It is at this point that your spiritual awakening begins, for fear has left that threshold. Many people may scoff at you, but once you have gone through your cycle of resistance, you begin to feel the unconditional love that is so much stronger than external judgment.

You remember now that there is important work to be done. You are here to assist your planet, which you can only understand once you have released your addiction to the third dimensional illusions. Through the thinning veil of illusion you can perceive and begin to enter the new paradigm of reality. In the third dimensional paradigm, REAL was comprised of third/fourth dimensional molecules organized into a physical form.

You knew this form was real because it offered resistance to your touch. You could see it with your physical eyes and heard it with your physical ears. This form had hard edges and familiar angles. However, your new mental operating system perceives energy patterns that feel alive to you. You do not know what these energies are, but you have a feeling that they are another reality, a life form or, maybe a Higher Being.

Your "feelings" are changing right along with you thoughts. "Feeling" used to mean emotions or your sense of touch. Now your feelings are similar to a new kind of perception that you experience through your mind. Furthermore, you now realize that your mind is not just in your body. In fact, both your thinking and your emotions seem to be emanating from above you. This above is not above in space, but above in frequency.

Those of you who have been awakened long

enough to become familiar with your new version of SELF, are hearing a call to put all that you know to use. You are tired of keeping quiet so "they" won't judge you. You want to talk about what is happening in your body and in your life. You want to share your new world with other people who are experiencing the same thing.

In other words, now that your Multidimensional Operating System is integrating into your third/fourth dimensional brain, heart and body, you KNOW you cannot go back. You don't know exactly where you are going, but you WILL find out. Unfortunately, you are not sure how you will find out because you are still "in-between" who you were and who you are becoming.

However, your ever-expanding Unity Consciousness is telling you that you are connected to everything and everyone. You are connected to the planet, as well. In fact, you ARE the planet. It is the realization that you are the planet that allows you to remember that you are also the Higher Beings that you are hearing, seeing, touching and following into the unknown.

You don't know where you are going, but you have remembered to follow the "feel" of unconditional love. How did you get from the frightened, disillusioned one to following the flow of unconditional love? You don't remember, and you are not looking back to find out.

Congratulations dear Earth Friends.

A New Home

Mytre
Ashtar Command

Suzanne Lie

The Restoration Chamber

MYTRE SPEAKS:

When I first arrived on the Arcturian Starship after "accidentally" navigating my Scout Ship with my mind, our society in the Pleiades was at the same stage of ascension as your Earthly society is now. However, when I arrived all I could do was tell the Arcturians that our planet was under attack. Shortly after, I was taken to the Restoration Chamber.

I would like to begin this message by telling you of my experience within the Chamber. As soon as I was in my chair and the door was closed, I was surrounded by total darkness. At first, I was a bit disconcerted by the darkness, but slowly an inner light began to awaken within me. I had never had an experience of perceiving this light before. It seemed to be coming from the top of my head.

The light began to move throughout my brain, as if it were looking for something. After an unknown period of time the source of the light seemed to settle into the very center of my brain. From there it projected a beam into my inner forehead, at which point I passed out.

When I awoke, I could see in the dark. I knew the room was still dark because I was seeing through a higher frequency of vision. I could pan-in or pan-out from what I saw without moving my head in any way. I also realized that I could see to either side, and even behind me, without moving my head. What I realize now is that I was seeing through my Third Eye.

Once I had a chance to "play" with my new vision, I began to feel an immense burning just above my heart. The burning sensation was so intense that I was paralyzed with pain. If I moved my body in any fashion, the pain escalated. On the other hand, if I totally relaxed into a calm, slow breath, the pain receded. Hence, I remained totally still for an unknown time.

I think I fell asleep, for it was not the same sensation as before when I passed out. When I returned to an awakened state the pain was gone, and I felt unbelievably filled with love. My wife and daughter came into my thoughts, and I immediately saw a picture of them in my mind. Later, much later, I learned that I had actually seen them.

I focused on our village with my mind to see if I could see anything, but all I could receive was an intense fatigue and sense of dread. I later learned that searching for love was an easier task than seeing fear and violence. I also learned that the reason for this discrepancy was for me to learn to follow the sensation of love during my inter-dimensional travels. Of course, at that time, I had no idea what glory my future would hold.

My pondering was interrupted by the opening of

the door to the Chamber, which opened quite on its own. I later learned that when the one in the chair resonated to a certain frequency, the door automatically opened. As I slowly stepped down from the chair, I felt a completely unique sensation course throughout my body.

I had no idea what that sensation was, but it was quite blissful. I later learned that my entire body had been re-calibrated to the fifth-dimensional frequency of resonance. However, I could only maintain the gift of higher resonance that I was given by the Arcturians by learning to be the Master of ALL my thoughts and emotions. This mastery was no easy task, but I did achieve it because the reward was so immense.

Once I found how to balance my new legs, I slowly walked through the door and out of the Chamber. I then entered a quiet corridor. The floor felt more like a cloud than the ground, but I was not sure if it was the floor or my new body. I later found that it was both. The corridor was empty, but I felt the thoughts of the crewmembers as if they were there with me.

The thoughts of so many people swirling through my mind gave me a headache and a feeling of nausea. I put my hand out to hold onto the wall for stability and was instantly overwhelmed by information regarding ALL the workings of the Ship. Fortunately, I heard a quiet instruction emanating from my heart (which was yet another novel experience) that instructed me to close my eyes and go deep into my own Core.

I was not sure what "going into my Core" meant, but I correctly imagined that it meant to find my own Center. When I focused on the Center of my self, I could find a place of peace and even quiet. Within that quiet I realized that I was hearing these voices from within myself rather than through my ears.

I found my Center again so that I could balance my body enough to stand on my own. I then gradually opened my eyes and saw the smiling face of an Arcturian. "Very good," It spoke. (Arcturians are androgynous even when they are wearing a form.) "Follow me," it said, as it led the way. It could tell that I was still disoriented and kept a slow pace.

At first I did not see much of the Ship, as I had to keep my eyes focused on the Arcturian to avoid further dizziness. However, as I continued to walk I became steadier on my new feet. I had a million questions to ask but knew that I had to respect their means of teaching me.

The Arcturian led me to a Debriefing Room, where I told them everything that was happening on my planet, as well as everything that happened to me on the Ship. After my meeting I was taken to my own quarters, shown how to operate the replicator to make myself some food, and encouraged to relax and get some sleep. I did everything I was asked to do, except sleep.

I tossed and turned and could not stop thinking

long enough to surrender to sleep. I had so many questions. Why did they leave me here alone? What was going to happen next? How were Mytria and my infant daughter? How was my planet? Did the Arcturians save them? And on, and on, and on…

Finally my door buzzed, and I invited an unknown Being to enter. I say "Being" because my unbidden communications revealed that there were Beings from all over the Galaxy aboard this Ship. Fortunately, when the door opened it was an Arcturian who entered. I had had enough surprises for a while.

With a slight smile, the Arcturian said, "How are you doing with mastery of your thoughts?"

Mastering Thought and Perceiving with Emotion

MYTRE CONTINUES:

When the Arcturian kindly mentioned my thinking, I had to laugh. I realized that my out-of-control thinking was partially because I had been recalibrated to a frequency of resonance that I had never experienced before.

I also recognized that I was frightened because my thoughts and emotions were out of alignment with my new body. I remembered the Elohim that Mytria and I had met within the Womb of the Mother long, long ago. However, I had never met an Arcturian, much less experienced a frequency rate of beingness that allowed me to perceive and interact with them.

"Good," spoke the Arcturian standing just inside my doorway. "You have correctly discerned that we took you to the Restoration Room to expand your resonance. You were taken there because you passed a major initiation of mastering your thoughts and perceiving with your emotions."

I had no idea what *perceiving with my emotions* meant, but I was very clear about my difficulty in mastering my thoughts. On the other hand, when I was flying the Ship with my mind, I had only one thought, and I felt that thought with every cell of my body.

"Follow me," the Arcturian directed, but I saw no movement of its mouth. Furthermore, I heard its message inside my heart instead of through my ears. However, the Arcturian did not explain what I was experiencing. With a knowing smile, it turned and walked away. I was very groggy from lack of sleep and intense anxiety, but I woke up quickly in my vain attempt to keep up with it.

For starters, the Arcturian did not actually walk. It moved just above the ground. In fact, I sensed that it could just blink itself to its destination, but was only using its present archaic locomotion for my benefit. I was clear that I had a lot to learn if I was to remain on this Starship.

The Arcturian guided me into what was likely a holosuite, because it was a huge area with a beautiful lake, warm sun, and a soft breeze that gently moved the leaves on the many trees. In fact, it was the exact area where I first met Mytria. With that realization, a wave of deep loneliness and sorrow rushed through me.

"You have been through a great change," the Arcturian said. "We have created a familiar place for you to rest and become accustomed to your new frequency of form. You may use your mind to call up anyone that you wish to visit."

"But, will they be real?" I asked.

"What do you mean by real?" The Arcturian queried.

I did not even know how to answer that question, so I stumbled around and said,

"You know, real in that it is not just my imagination."

"Everything is your imagination," the Arcturian said as it turned and left the lake, the holosuite, or was it *the reality*?

Unfortunately, I could not ask these questions because the Arcturian was suddenly gone. Obviously, I was on the fast track of learning, and I had to stop questioning and start remembering what had happened to me on the Ship.

Therefore, I started to call up the illusion, hologram or reality of my shipmates to ask them what they had seen. That was when I remembered that they must be on the Starship too. Before I had a chance to ponder that question, all three of my crewmates, including the one who had died, appeared before me.

I was overwhelmed to see someone who I knew was dead standing in front of me. Maybe he was a hologram, but if he was, I didn't want to be the one to break it to him. "We brought you some food," they said. We sat down on a flat rock and ate our simple food while we all pretended that this experience was normal, and I tried to figure out if it was real

Is It Real?

MYTRE SPEAKS:

After I ate familiar food with my crewmates, we stripped down and swam in the lake. Then, we lay down on the warm rock and talked about nothing. We told jokes, laughed and finally feel asleep on the warm rocks. When I awoke, the sun was low on the horizon and my friends were gone.

Suddenly, I was engulfed by the deep sorrow about leaving my beloved family that I had not been able to feel. I was alone now, so I could cry like a baby, and I did. As I cried, images from being on the Mother's land with Mytria, laughing with her, and making love filled my heart.

Slowly, I realized that those images were stronger than the feeling of grief, and I began to focus on the feel of the images. As I allowed the feeling of deep friendship, love and fun to fill my body, I began to understand what the Arcturian meant by "perceiving with emotion."

When my emotion was sad, all I could perceive was that I was alone on a rock that I once shared with my beloved Mytria. However, as I gave my sorrow a voice, my perceptions began to change. In my mind's eye I actually saw Mytria beside me, and the feeling of love filling my body. Finally content, I looked out towards the setting Sun and saw my

SELF.

I don't know how to explain how I saw myself, as I saw it with the emotion of Bliss. I had released my loneliness and deep sorrow and replaced it with the FEEL of love for another. Then, once I felt love for another, I was able to love my SELF. By SELF, I mean, the self that is ONE with the SELF that is ONE.

At that time, that sounded like a poor sentence, but gradually I began to understand what it meant. I was creating the hologram with my thoughts, just like the Arcturian said I would. I called forth my friend and gave life to my friend who had died. I hung out with them on a sunny day because I needed to feel like a "normal" guy relaxing with his buddies. Finally, I fell asleep, as I could no longer believe the fantasy that I had created.

With the loss of my illusion, I had to face my truth. Fear and sorrow came fast, and love and happiness came in a slow, but enduring manner. When I allowed my emotions to speak to me, I could see the truth around me. Much to my surprise, that truth included the fact that my sorrow was not just for my family.

I was mourning the loss of all that I had held to be true, honest and real. Now that I realized that my real world was an illusion, all I could perceive was the truth. With that final realization, the lake vanished, the rock vanished, the trees vanished and the setting sun revealed the door out of the holosuite.

I knew that walking through that door was acknowledging that everything that I had ever known, done, had and experienced was an illusion. Through the door was my true SELF. Yes, of course, this SELF was within me, but through the door I would learn how to remember who I really am.

I stared at the flat door on the empty wall for a very long time. I knew that I no longer had a choice. Once I had moved our small Ship with my mind, everything changed because I had changed. Then, when I left the Restoration Chamber, I began to BE my truth, which terrified me.

I stood up and walked toward the door. With my head held high, I walked through the door and followed the awaiting Arcturian who greeted me with an open heart. No words were needed, for now I could read its mind.

As my Arcturian friend (they don't have names in the manner that I was used to) led me through the corridor, it started to float higher and higher above the floor. I know that it was encouraging me to do the same, but my doubts were louder than my belief in my SELF.

With that thought, the Arcturian turned around and stared into my face. Gradually, a small golden light grew within me. In fact, it felt as if it was gently rising above the threshold of my inner doubt.

I know that sentence does not make sense, but my doubt was not infinite. It was strong within the part of me that still held fear, the part of me that held the dark. However, this golden ball was rising above that fear and filling me with light.

Yes, of course, this is the Sun that revealed the door out of the holosuite and into my SELF. The Arcturian read my imagistic mind and spoke to me in an image more powerful than words. I could feel tears rolling down my face, but they were tears of joy. I threw back my head and opened my heart to the growing joy within me.

I raised my arms up and out to surrender my heart to…what? I did not know, but the sensation of surrender felt wonderful. I closed my eyes and the surrender turned into bliss and the bliss turned into a total quiet, a complete calm and a sensation of floating.

And then the Arcturian said, "Open your eyes."

I did not want to open my eyes. I was concerned that if I saw the outside world I lose these marvelous, healing sensations.

"Open your eyes now," I heard with a sense of urgency.

Reluctantly, I opened my eyes and saw the ceiling of the Corridor inches away from my nose.

I was so startled that I lost my concentration and started to fall.

"STOP!"

Much to my surprise, my fall was halted by the Arcturians firm words. I held the feeling of command in my mind, as I repeated, "STOP" until I could lower my feet to the ground.

With a sense of pride mixed with

embarrassment, I looked up into the Arcturian's eyes.

"Now is the time to start your lessons," said the Arcturian with its mind.

A New Home

Arcturian Lessons

PART V

Suzanne Lie

Signature Frequencies

MYTRE SPEAKS:

When I awoke the next morning I was so excited that I couldn't get dressed quickly enough. (Morning was a chosen cycle rather the rising of the Sun, as we were in outer space. Thus, it was always "night" outside the Ship.) I was in such a hurry to dress that I put my jacket on inside-out and had to take even more "time" to take my jacket off and put it back on correctly. (Time was another decided event as the Arcturians live within the ever-present NOW.)

I restrained myself from running through the Corridors to the collective Mess Hall. The Mess Hall is for the non-Arcturian crew, as Arcturians do not eat food. When I entered the busy room I was surprised to see my two crewmates. No, my third friend was not resurrected. I walked swiftly over to them and embraced them both.

It appears that they were waiting for me. We all went to get our food, which was an experience in itself. Since there were members of the Ship from all over our Galaxy and beyond, we were presented with a vast array of food. I chose a simple Pleiadian breakfast dish, as did my two friends. However, the humorous discussion about our many culinary choices set a welcomed tone of camaraderie and happiness.

My friends were very happy because they were about to take a Ship back to our new Homeworld in the Pleiades. They expected that I would be joining them and were very disappointed to hear that I would stay with the Arcturians. I was, of course, struck with great guilt when they asked how I could stay away from Mytria and our new baby. They also wanted to know if I had clearance from our Commander to remain with the Arcturians.

When I told them that I had gained the proper clearance, I also had to tell them that I could not share why. I hated to keep a secret from my friends with whom I had just shared a near-death experience, but how could I tell them what I was learning? Our conversation soon degraded from friendly camaraderie to an uncomfortable discussion about their return and my staying.

Finally, I had to make an excuse to leave, as the guilt of staying away from my family and my Homeworld was overpowering. Instead of the welcoming warm embraces of our first greeting, we ended with a rather stiff handshake, as I tried to slowly leave the room. "Well, so much for my first glorious day of training," I thought as I left the room.

A huge black cloud was over my head as I walked, face looking down, through the corridor. In fact, I was so absorbed in my self-pity that I almost ran into my Arcturian mentor. Running into a Light Being is a very unique experience, as I literally walked INTO it.

When I did so, I was surrounded by such illumination and unconditional love that I fell onto the floor as if I had been wounded. In actuality, my wounded self fell to the floor. At the same time, I could feel another part of me; I guess it was my own Lightbody, rise up above me. I felt like two extreme polarities of one person.

The confusion of my wounded self and the enlightenment of my Lightbody was such a unique experience that I almost passed out with the effort to expand my consciousness to these extremes. Fortunately, the Arcturian came to my assistance by reaching down and gently touching the back of the wounded one's heart.

Instantly, my Light SELF rushed into my physical heart and with no effort, I stood up. When I did so, I realized that the Arcturian was floating above the ground and its face was out of vision. In fact, its face was more of a radiant light with two focus points that I imagined were its eyes.

It was talking with me telepathically, but I could not hear. My physical distance from its heart and eyes made me believe that I could not hear its telepathic message. Of course that thought was nonsense, but it was the thought that came into me.

Was that thought actually the message? Then I realized that the Arcturian was telling me to levitate myself up to the level in which I could be closer to its head and heart. Yes, levitate, I told myself. I tried to remember how I did that before, but I couldn't remember how.

After I tried and tried, I became frustrated. No! I became angry. How can this Arcturian expect so much of me? I have only been on this infinitely huge ship a few days. I have just gotten a new body and deserted my family and my Homeworld so that they can teach me to fly!!!

There was my guilt, peppered with anger. What had I done? Had I made the right decision? Was I good enough to fulfill their huge expectations of me? And on and on... I then heard, VERY LOUDLY,

"How are you doing with mastering of your thinking?"

Arcturian humor! They had the ability to be funny. The concept of this immense Light Being hovering over my head and making a joke sent me into uncontrolled laughter. The laughing released the anger, released the guilt, and released the sorrow, which was the foundation for the guilt and anger. The laughing became more controllable and slowly morphed into a sensation of joy.

I closed my eyes in appreciation of the joy, which then expanded the joy into love. At this point the Arcturian touched the very top of my head, and I felt the most extreme bliss I had ever experienced. The bliss continued until I bumped my head on the ceiling of the Corridor. Did I hear the Arcturian laugh?

I fell to the ground in a rather undignified manner and looked up to see the Arcturian smiling.

It reached down to touch me, and we *beamed* into another area of the Ship. This means of transportation was quite exhilarating. I felt no experience of moving. I call it "beaming to another area," because it seemed to me that I was one place, then my eyes closed for a blink of "time," and my eyes opened to a different environment.

In this case, I assumed it was another holosuite for we were standing on a rock cliff looking at constellations and galaxies in space that I had never seen. "Where are we?" I asked. "Are we in another holosuite?" He instructed me to blink again, and I opened my eyes to the familiar vision of the constellations above my Homeworld in the Pleiades.

I tried to be polite when I said, "Is this a hologram or is it real?"

"Is there a difference?" was the response that I heard.

I would have to think before I asked my next question. Or, maybe I should not ask any questions. I had learned so far that a question answered just led to another question. Therefore, I decided to wait and allow the Arcturian to continue with whatever point it was making.

Therefore, I watched silently as many beautiful visions of constellations and galaxies filled my vision. As the beauty overtook my thoughts, I began to realize that each vision created a different sensation within my Heart.

At that point, I again saw the first constellation

that I was shown. However, this time I remembered to FEEL every sensation that filled my body, every emotion that arose from those sensations and to listen to every thought that came into my mind.

We went through the cycle of constellations and galaxies many times. Each time, I was able to FEEL the sensations, emotions and thoughts that were initiated by each vision. It was then that I heard the word, "Signature Frequency."

Yes, I got it. Each world has a Signature Frequency. By then, I had recognized some of the stars, constellations and galaxies and realized how the Signature Frequency gave infinitely more information than the titles that we had given them.

I turned toward the Arcturian to tell it that I understood, but it was gone. However, I heard a clear message in my heart that I was to stay there until I had memorized every Signature Frequency.

Suzanne Lie

Inside the Arcturian

MYTRE SPEAKS:

I absorbed the Celestial Signature Frequencies for so long that I could no longer keep my eyes open. To my surprise, I could absorb them in a completely different manner when my eyes were closed. It was as if the perceptions of my new, fifth dimensional body only kicked in when I was not using my physical vision. Also, an interesting sound that was beyond my hearing with my eyes open began to resonate throughout my Lightbody.

This resonance, along with the changing light images striking my inner vision, set my new form into a spin. At first I barely noticed it and thought I was just dizzy from concentrating for so long. However, I was not concentrating then, and the dizziness quickly transformed into a buzzing sensation that ran through my entire form. I understand why it made me dizzy at first, because this sensation traveled in ever-expanding circles out from my body.

These circles of sensations traveled out at the same time that they traveled deeper and deeper into my form. As if that was not enough, there was a wave sensation that started to flow up and down my form. I found I could no longer keep my balance enough to stand or even sit, so I lay down flat on the hard rock on which I had been standing.

Once I changed the angle of my body, the sensations also adjusted so that the waves, which were once perpendicular to the rock became horizontal with the rock. In this manner, the waves continued to move up and down my spine. Simultaneously, the ever-expanding circles were moving deeper and deeper into the rock and higher and higher above me.

There seemed to be a rhythm to the circles and the waves, so I decided to match my breathing to that rhythm. WOW, just two or three breaths and I took off. I am not sure which "I" took off, but I was no longer lying on a rock looking into the Cosmos. Instead, I was flowing through the Cosmos.

I say that I was "flowing," rather than flying, as I was not moving any of my body parts. It was more like I was flowing with an invisible stream. I knew that I must be moving in my consciousness and that my body was probably still lying on the rock. However, I was so enjoying my experience that I didn't want to do anything to alter it.

There was a glint of a question about whether I was in a superior holoprogram, or if this experience was real. Fortunately, just before the doubt set in, I heard the Arcturians words, "Is there a difference?" If I created this part of the holoprogram with my thoughts, or if I created this reality, I was the creator in both cases.

An inner voice reminded me to stop analyzing, as it lowered my consciousness and diminished my experience. To my credit, I actually stopped thinking and surrendered more deeply into my journey. At this point of surrender, either I fell asleep or went into a deeper state of consciousness. Actually, isn't sleep and surrender the same? Either way, my logical thinking stopped.

I stopped analyzing, stopped questioning and just LET GO. It was as if I heard a silent snap and took off like a rocket at about a 45-degree angle towards my right. I began to resonate so quickly that all thought and/or emotion were impossible. I was no longer wearing a body. I was pure consciousness. However, my consciousness had more awareness than it ever did when a humanoid form restrained it.

Then my Essence shot out like a star burst, and I was fully aware of every perception from a myriad of different viewpoints. I do not know how I did this, but I knew that this experience could only happen when my consciousness resonated to a very high frequency of reality.

What happened next was even more surprising. Each of the starburst points became a different expression of my total self. Within the NOW of the ONE, I could simultaneously perceive, experience and interact with each of these versions of my SELF.

Suddenly, as if I had crossed some invisible threshold, my experience became too much for me. I felt like a Starship that was going too fast for the Ship to maintain its integrity. I did not want to end this experience, but I began to wonder what would happen if I didn't culminate this adventure.

"STOP!"

I heard within. It was the Arcturian speaking. I knew this because I had recognized its Signature Frequency.

"Stop, slowly," I again heard within.

However, since I didn't how I had started this journey, I did not know how to end it. I was going faster and faster and starting to feel completely out of control, which frightened me.

"Open your eyes, NOW," The Arcturian said.

I opened my eyes quickly, as if by some defense reflex. Then the dizziness came on full force. I was spinning so fast that I could not tell up from down and right from left. I was completely disoriented and on the verge of—I don't know what—when I felt a warm light around me.

Instantly, I was calm, safe, centered and inside the Arcturian???

I tried to move out of it, as it did not want to invade its body, but I heard it say, "Just sleep. That is enough for now."

I woke up the next "morning" in my bunk feeling like a new person. How could I wrap my mind around what had happened? I started to repeat my old question of, "Was that real or just a dream?"

I got my own answer this time, which was, "Is there a difference?"

Waiting for the Light

MYTRE CONTINUES:

My "new person" decided to go to the group Mess Hall rather than eat alone in my cabin. Little did I know what would happen. I took my sonic shower, even though I did not want to wash any of the Arcturian energy off my body. However, it was a lifelong habit to bathe in the morning, so I did.

While I was in the shower, I wondered how many of my lifelong habits would leave me now. I had no idea that my life would take me to this experience. No wait, I had no CONSCIOUS idea that my life would go this way. But there was always a "something" that wiggled around in the back of my mind that there was "more." I had no idea what this "more" was, but the feeling grew as I matured.

Now, I was on an Arcturian Starship, and I had just experienced being inside of an Arcturian. My mind was reeling at the concept of existing inside of another Being, when a small anger began to grow within me. "Where is that coming from?" I asked my self. I pushed the anger away, got dressed and went to the Mess Hall.

As soon as I got there, I knew that it was a bad idea. I looked around at all the "normal" people, at least they were normal to their world, and knew that

I did not fit. I no longer fit in my old world, nor did I fit in this world. I looked about the room and wondered how many of them had experienced what I had. Then, I reprimanded my self for being elitist. But, I didn't feel better than them. I just felt, out of the loop.

How, and with whom, could I share what had been happening to me? On the other hand, how could I keep this all bottled up inside? With that last thought, I began to feel such pressure in my body that I felt like I would burst. NO, I did not want to be so alone. It was hard enough to leave my family, to abandon my Village, to not return home with my crewmates. They would be received as heroes, and I was the one who had saved the day!

Where did that arrogant thought come from? Obviously, I was not fit for public life right now. I turned in such a hurry that I bumped into a tall Antarian. When he growled at me, as Antarians often do, I yelled at him to get out my way. I pushed him in a combative way. If he were not the better man, we would have had a fight right there in the Mess Hall.

Mortified by my behavior, I literally ran from the Mess Hall, out the door and through the corridors in a desperate attempt to find solitude. I was so angry, afraid and sad that I never considered returning to my cabin.

"As the Cycle completes, that which is left in the dark must be released into the Light," came the voice of the Arcturian inside my head.

"Where are you?" I yelled in an embarrassing manner.

Quickly realizing what I had done, I tried to apologize. Unfortunately, only more anger could be found. I did not voice this anger, but since the Arcturian read my mind better than I could, I might as well have screamed it.

There was no answer. I knew that I had not listened to what the Arcturian had already said, so why would it tell me more? I realized that in my fit of "unconscious" anger, I had unconsciously run to the holosuite. Since I was there, I might as well go inside. The same program of Signature Frequencies was running. Actually, I am sure the Arcturian could see in it's NOW that I would end up here and would need the familiarity of something, even if it was a holoprogram.

I sat down on the familiar rock and pondered what the Arcturian meant by, "As the Cycle completes…" I was aware that a cycle of my life had definitely completed and that I would never be the same person, but why the anger? Well, of course, it was because I felt out of control. As a long time warrior, being out of control was the most frightening thing, and fear had to be transformed into anger if a warrior was to survive.

Perhaps, it was the cycle of being a warrior that was ending, for I would never be able to take another life now. Maybe I had to drain out the last remnant of the anger that allowed me to survive the fear that I could not allow myself to feel while in battle.

"Do you still feel angry?" came the voice of the Arcturian inside my head.

My first reaction was to get angry that the Arcturian would not talk to me "face to face like a man!" Of course, there was that combative anger again. The Arcturian was not a "man." In fact, I wasn't even sure if it was a humanoid. However, I realized that I did not want to get angry at this amazing Being who was teaching me so much. In fact, I began to feel very remorseful about my behavior, as well as my negative thoughts and uncontrolled emotions.

"It is important to release that which you no longer need," came the familiar, loving voice.

The concept of not needing fear, anger and sorrow was mind-shattering. How would I protect myself without my fear, fight my battles without anger and mourn my losses without sorrow?

"Do you still enjoying creating those aspects of your reality?" the Arcturian calmly asked, as if I had a choice.

"You always have a choice," the Arcturian responded to my thoughts. "YOU are the creator of your reality."

Wait a minute here, I thought. Did the Arcturian just say that I created the lifetime of war, the endangerment of our village and the loss of my crewmate? The anger began to rise within me like a firestorm.

I wanted to yell at the Arcturian for blaming me

for everything that had happened to my world when I suddenly felt a sweet, inner-love wrap around me like a warm blanket. For the first time in my entire life I felt safe, not safe because I was protecting, but safe because I was protected.

"Dear Mytre, this feeling is what you have offered to others. It lies just beneath your anger. After all, how could you give to others what you did not have within your self?"

"But, I thought that feeling of safety came from you," I queried.

"No Mytre, the safety that you felt came from within yourself. We only amplified that which was already there."

I knew that I felt anger, fear, sorrow and even love. But I had never thought that I had felt safe. With that thought, my mind became filled with images of childhood with my beloved parents. Our world was under attack, but they never let me feel it. They protected me from their fear, their anger and even their sorrow. When they were with me, they always made me feel safe and loved.

I began to sob, not from sorrow, but from gratitude for the wonderful gift that they had invisibly given me. They sacrificed everything to give me what I needed and told me continuously that I was special and that I would do great things one day.

But while I was away at school yet another bombing killed them. I was so devastated that I forgot about the safety they had given me and replaced it with sorrow, fear and hate. I started sobbing inconsolably when I realized that I had forgotten their gifts. I had also forgotten who I had become.

"You have become the great, Awakening One that you are in this NOW. Your parents gave you the safety you needed to gain the courage to be a warrior. Now, you must call upon that courage to fight your own inner battle," spoke the Arcturian.

"However, you will not fight this inner battle with anger and fear, for any emotion that you express is amplified by your expression. Therefore, our dear Mytre, you will fight this inner battle with unconditional love for your SELF."

For what seemed like a lifetime, I was silent both in my words and in my thoughts and emotions. This deep silence comforted me and led me to my Core. I had never thought of having a Core, but there it was. It was a place within the center of my body that was absolutely quiet. There were no thoughts, no feelings, and no images—nothing!

There was only the silence of the darkest night before the dawn. I had just re-lived my darkest night, but it was not yet dawn. I think the Arcturian turned off the holoprogram, for the darkness in the room was as absolute as the darkness in my Core.

Fear wanted to pull me away from this deep, inner-void. Sorrow wanted to fill it with its unshed tears. Anger wanted to fight its way into the dawn. But love — unconditional love — felt safe and could patiently wait for the light.

And so, I waited!

Bubbles Of Reality

MYTRE SPEAKS:

As I sat in the completely darkened holosuite, focusing on the void within my Core, I began to have sensations in my body. At first, my back and legs were stiff from sitting in the same position for an untold period of time. Then my arms, shoulders and neck hurt, and my face twitched. Eventually even my eyelashes and hair seemed to hurt.

Finally, the uncomfortable sensations ceased, and I began to experience my body as a flexible cord that was being stretched to its fullest length. At this point, the cord became increasingly warm and began to unravel. I was watching the imagistic language, trying to translate every image.

I believed that the pain and discomfort represented how my Soul felt while limited in the confines of this physical vehicle. Once I allowed that concept into my mind, my consciousness shifted to the perspective of being above my body.

At the same time that I was above my body, I also felt my form around me. Interestingly, I was having the sensation that I was *wearing* my body, rather than being *in* my body. In fact, I wondered if my body was flesh and blood or another creation of the holosuite. I then began to feel as though there was a third version of me who appeared as a cloud emanation who was floating far above me.

There was also a version of me that I could sense, but could not see. Nonetheless, I heard this *me* saying to an unseen friend, "I just had a very interesting dream. I was on a vessel in the sky. I was sitting alone in a dark room while this immense Being of light watched over me. I don't know how I knew I was in a vessel. In fact, I didn't know what that huge vehicle was or how I ended up there."

Then a curtain closed across my mind, and I saw my home on the Pleiades. I saw the beautiful green that covered our world. However our homes were quite different from what I remembered. Each home was of living crystal, which could change shape and size with mere thought. Even though this world was different than mine, I felt very homesick when that image began to fade.

"Wait, I like this vision. I don't want to leave here."

"You never leave a reality," said the Arcturian. "You just change your intention. All programs of reality are infinitely strung together. It is just that you can only take so much before your brain loses focus. It is best to paint your thoughts, so that you will not forget them."

"Paint my thoughts? " I began. I wanted to ask more, but when I looked at my body, I was a female from yet another reality. However, I was an artist and was using a small brush on a huge square of white material."

Unfortunately, I did not stay there either.

Instead, my mind wandered around realities like it was shopping at a store. Just as I got used to visiting one reality, I was led to another. My awareness swept though reality after reality, as if I was searching for something, or someone.

I knew that I was creating these experiences, as I could hear the Arcturian reminding me that I was the creator of my life. At first I was a Pleiadian in all my realities, but when I surrendered to this process, I could experience myself as many other races.

I saw realities in which I was Antarian, Sirian, Tau Cetian, Andromedan, Lemurian and Atlantian. There it was. Atlantis was the reality I was searching for. However, that reality was in a time frame far in the future of my Pleiadian life.

It was then that I began to experience realities that were on totally different Timelines than the one in which I thought I was living. With this realization, I began jumping through myriad timelines. I would settle into one time, then just an instant later; I was in a completely different reality in a totally different Timeline. Then, I began randomly shifting through realities in times and places that I had never known existed.

I was wondering what the point of this vision was when I heard the Arcturian say, "BE Careful." What was I to be careful about? Then I found out. The worlds began to course through my mind faster and faster until they all blended into a united flow of life.

The realities spun so fast that they started moving in inner, concentric circles as they traveled deeper and deeper into my Core. My dark Core was now filled with bright light and more activity than I could contain. I felt a sudden upward force, as if a fountain had been turned on.

Suddenly, the many realities joined into one force of energy that rushed back up my core like an erupting volcano. The energy shot out through my crown like a huge fountain of light. I could see higher and higher frequencies of reality as the light was disseminated into the dark room, filling it with brilliant images of a myriad of realities.

Then unexpectedly, everything stopped. The images froze in place, and all the worlds ceased their rotation. Everything in the room became completely still, except for the image of me. However, this image of me was without a form. I was a swirling energy field, which was the only source of movement within the entire room. All the many worlds which once revealed life, thought, movement and emotion were totally still.

I traveled from image to image observing the worlds that were stopped in mid-motion. Wars stopped with unexploded bombs in the air, parades halted with marchers stretching out a leg held in preparation for the next step, and Starships hovered motionless in space. Every person, place and thing was totally still.

"What happened?" I asked the unseen Arcturian.

"You left time."

Somehow, I totally understood that concept. I peeked into the many realities and realized that they were moving, but so slowly in comparison to me that they appeared to be still. I looked at my flowing form of pure energy surrounded by the myriad bubbles of reality, floating through silent streams of light.

"What if I went backward, and instead of the realities flowing out from my core, they flowed back into my core? Would I travel back in time?" I telepathically asked the Arcturian.

"Try it and see," was its response.

I thought about trying to get back in time by reversing the process that took me out of time, but wondered if I really wanted to do that. After pondering that question, I decided I wanted more freedom from time. Time had always been a bit of a burden.

Hence, I decided to experience more of my formless state. However, I did peek into several of the surrounding bubbles of reality to see if I had a body in any of them. I did this, just in case I could not remember how to get back into form without joining a reality. Somewhere in this room had to be the bubble of reality in which I was in a holosuite on an Arcturian Starship learning about time.

There were so many realities that I didn't want to look into them all. Of course I could find the Signature Frequency of that specific reality. However, to do so I would have to remember how I was feeling, what I was thinking and who I was being while resonating to that Signature Frequency.

I would like to say that I closed my eyes, but being a formless swirl of light, I had no eyes. Hence, I could only go into my imagistic memory. I remembered how I felt in the room when I entered the void of my core. I felt the total darkness of the void within and the dark room around me. The darkness actually brought a strange comfort. Yes, it was the comfort of having a form.

I was greatly enjoying being formless, but was also a bit concerned that I would not be able to return to a body, just in case I wanted to. I remembered the feel of my body after I sat immobile for an unknown period of time. Time, it was already becoming a choice rather than a symbol for being alive.

I was outside of time and felt completely alive, vibrant and free. The juxtaposition of feeling myself in a body which was cramped, tired and in pain, pulled my energy field toward a certain one of the many bubbles of reality. I did not resist and allowed the images and sensation to direct my flow. Then, I found myself interfacing with one of the reality bubbles and decided to look inside.

Bad idea! I was instantly pulled into that reality. The room was dark, and I was inside of a dense form that hurt in every imaginable fashion. My mind was racing with undirected thoughts, my emotions were only dimly controlled and the body was so dense that it felt as though my energy had hit a dense wall.

I tried to pull back from the onrushing density, but it was too late. I was pulled into the darkness, into the thoughts, into the emotions and into the body. "Ouch!" was my first comment. I spoke? I had a voice and thoughts were in me rather than around me. I was no longer a flowing energy field, and my body was the dense form with which I had just collided.

I tried to get out of that body, as it no longer felt like *me*. But it was too late. I was trapped in time once again. However, now that I had experienced the freedom of being in the NOW I was determined free myself again.

Time and Dimensions of Reality

MYTRE SPEAKS:

After my experience of leaving time, my life would be forever changed. It appears that by leaving time I had passed an important initiation and was ready to continue my studies elsewhere. However, I was not told where. Since I would be going into an "advanced program," I knew it was important for me to refresh my memory about the structure of time and dimensions.

Until I emerged from the Restoration Chamber I had lived within the concept of time. However even on a physical world, time is relative because it is measured by the rotation of a planet. One complete rotation of the planet signifies a day and a complete rotation of the planet around the Sun signifies a year. Since the many planets and Solar Systems that we visited had varying sizes, the rotations were different as was the concept of a *day* and a *year*.

Therefore, I knew that time was not a static measurement and was relative to the world we were visiting. However, I did not know that time was different in different dimensions until I came to the Arcturian Ship. As soon as I arrived on the ship I was aware that time was different, which was because the ship instantly put me into a state of fourth dimensional consciousness.

However, even when I arose from the Restoration Chamber with a higher frequency of body, my force of habit kept me thinking in a sequential manner like most of the crewmembers and visitors to the ship. I had the habit of third dimensional thinking even though the ship actually resonated more to the fourth dimension. However, once I "left time" everything changed. Leaving time freed me from sequential thinking, and I began to think and perceive more than one thing at a "time."

This shift in perception of reality was quite disturbing, and likely part of the reason why I was ready for advanced training. For one thing, because I was holding many thoughts within the NOW of "no-time" I had great difficulty speaking. Of course the Arcturian could read my mind before I tried to put my many concurrent thoughts into a sentence. Nevertheless, I could not talk to others.

Moreover, I could see the fourth dimensional aura of everyone and everything on the Ship. People thought that I was avoiding them because I carefully walked around their aura. Also, I knew what people would say before they said it. In fact, I think I knew what they were going to say even before they thought it. I telepathically asked the Arcturian if this is what is was like for It and I instantly telepathically heard "YES."

It was quite difficult for me to become accustomed to my multidimensional perception, which in my case meant that I could see the third and the fourth dimension simultaneously. The Arcturian could tell that I was struggling and actually sat me down to have a talk.

"Mytre," began the Arcturian, "We see that your anxiety is building because you are unaccustomed to your new, multidimensional perception. As you know, we usually teach you through experience, but we realize that what you need now is information. Therefore, we will tell you about time and dimensions.

"Time on the third, fourth and fifth dimension is quite different. We remind you that the second, third and fourth dimensions are within the paradigm of time and separate physical forms. On the other hand, dimensions five, six, and seven are within the paradigm of the NOW and Unity Consciousness in mutable forms.

"In the eighth through twelfth dimensions all consciousness exists as ONE within the infinite NOW. No form is necessary in these worlds, and bodies are only worn when a Being is inter-dimensionally traveling in the lower dimensional worlds.

"A primary function of time in the third dimension is to create the illusion of separation. If it takes a long time for you to travel to visit a person, then you know that there is a great deal of space between you. Hence, the third dimension is the realm of *time and space*. As you have noted in your galactic travels, third dimensional time is specific to each planet.

"The most common means of experiencing the fourth dimension is through dreams or meditations, or while being on one of our Starships. Fourth dimensional time is much faster than third dimensional time. For example, you could have a dream while a certain song is playing on your third dimensional radio throughout the entire dream. Then, you wake up to find the song only half over. The song was only 3 minutes long, whereas your dream encompassed many years of experiences.

"Furthermore, in the fourth dimension it does not take *time* to travel from one place to another. You may find yourself in one place, than instantly switch to a new location. Also, you can change your shape within a fourth dimensional dream, vision. You could be a person, then instantly shift into a wolf, then back into a human.

"Therefore, a function of time in the fourth dimension is to confuse your third dimensional thinking enough for you to begin to release your attachment to time. Your dream and meditation life also allows you to release your attachment to your current third dimensional form. In your fourth dimensional realities you can change forms many times throughout one dream and/or meditation.

"Furthermore, your consciousness is very different in the fourth dimension than it is in the third dimension. In the physical world your consciousness is something that keeps you awake to the physical world. Conversely, in your dreams and meditations, your consciousness is the component of your Astral Body in which you can travel free of all physical limitation.

"Also, your state of consciousness greatly influences how you perceive the passage of time. For example, when you are engaged in a creative venture and/or doing something that you love, there is little sense of the passage of time. On the other hand, time moves very slowly when you are doing something that you perceive as boring, difficult or feels like *work*. Conversely, when you are engaged in an activity that you love or that is a creative expression of your true SELF, time seems to stop.

"Do you see how time is not real? Time is created to organize your thinking to match the matrix of a third dimensional planet. Once you shift your consciousness into a fourth dimensional thinking, your sensation of time is greatly altered. Then, when you experience fifth dimensional consciousness you are able to move beyond time completely and experience the NOW.

"Time is NOT the NOW, as the NOW is NOT a frozen moment of time. The Now of the fifth dimension indicates that you have aligned your consciousness with higher frequencies of reality. You have created this alignment by focusing your full intention and attention on a higher dimension of reality. However if you are involved in a higher dimensional NOW, and then your focus your attention on time, your consciousness will fall out of the experience of NOW.

"When your consciousness returned to the time-bound realities of the lower worlds, you fell out of the experience of NOW. Therefore, your experience of no-time ended once your thoughts returned to your time-bound reality on the ship. Then, your fourth dimensional energy field collapsed into the sensations of your aching, physical form, and your fifth dimensional state of the NOW was lost.

"Remember Mytre, in order to release the limitations of time, focus your attention on the NOW, and use your emotions to perceive your reality via imagistic, sensate pictures. By thinking and speaking via images, your consciousness can travel in circular patterns that weave in and out of interacting patterns. This point of focus will gradually free your energy field from the limitations of time.

"Speaking and thinking in an imagistic manner that is free of time markers such as distance, limitations, separation, gender and polarities will greatly assist you to break the habit of time. Also, if you fully partake in every moment of your present and release all thoughts of the past and future, you will slowly calibrate your thought patterns to the NOW of the fifth dimensional and beyond.

"Do you understand what we are saying?"

I had to think about whether or not I understood what I had just been told. Yes, I remembered that my journey beyond time ended when I thought about my uncomfortable physical form. These thoughts stopped my flow through the circular patterns of the bubbles of reality and set me on the search for my third/fourth dimensional reality.

To be totally honest with myself, I only sought that body because I was becoming frightened by a completely novel experience. I decided then that I would choose to recognize any fearful emotions and instantly release them. I knew that I was going into an even greater initiation and would need to call upon all my courage to remain centered within my Higher Frequency SELF.

If I could not be the master of my own thinking and emotions, how could I visit the higher dimensions of reality in which we were all ONE within the NOW? Therefore, I looked at the Arcturian and answered,

"Yes. I understand what you are saying."

Journey To the Mothership
PART VI

Suzanne Lie

The Arrival

MYTRE SPEAKS:

Early the next morning I was told to pack a few belongings and go to Launching Bay 7 to board a Shuttlecraft. I was not informed of my destination. I was not surprised by this order. I quickly prepared a small bag and went directly to the Launching Bay.

When I arrived, I was greeted by one of my friends who had a very interesting look on his face. My guess was that he was excited for me, which was affirmed when he said, "Congratulation," when I started to board the Shuttle. I had no time to question him, as the door was quickly closed behind me, and I was left the only passenger in the small Ship.

I sat there for a while wondering what my friend had meant when I heard the familiar telepathic message from the Arcturian saying, "Welcome Aboard."

I followed my instincts and found my dear friend the Arcturian waiting for me to pilot the craft. I had learned to release all questions, so when the Arcturian dialed in the co-ordinates of our destination, I started the Shuttlecraft and began our journey.

As I have said before, it is difficult to determine time while in space, and Arcturian Shuttle Craft did not bother with such archaic equipment as a clock. Therefore, I settled into the NOW of enjoying being in Space again. After many moments of the NOW, for we were traveling free of the limitations of time, I saw a huge light in the distance.

At first, the light appeared formless, which was because my mind had to adjust to the concept of perceiving a Mothership that was as large as a small planet. However, since my consciousness was prepared for a journey into the unknown, the LIGHT quickly began to take on a form. The form appeared to be a bright circular light within an orb, which was within another orb.

"We cloak our Ships in this fashion to adjust humanity's perception to consciously, or unconsciously, perceive these shapes," explained the Arcturian. Fear of the unknown is humanity's greatest fear. Hence, we are making ourselves known in a manner where one can *use their imagination* to see a Starship in the orbs, or simply ignore the image and keep their 'nose to the grindstone.'

"We also hide our Spaceships in the clouds of a planet's atmosphere for the grounded ones to ignore or perceive. Either way, these configurations become more familiar. Thus, they no longer elicit the fear of perceiving the *unknown*. There is much that is unknown to your current state of consciousness, and we wish to prepare you by guiding you to intermingle your Energy Field with ours. In this manner, you are calibrating your observations to a higher perspective of perception.

"Our Mothership holds the consciousness of myriad life forms from all over the Milky Way Galaxy and beyond. Also, the Mothership is so vast that thousands of beings can be on totally different parts of our Ship, and there would still be many unvisited areas. Since all our Motherships are biological, different areas morph and change to meet the needs of its myriad, different inhabitants. We do not think of our Ship as an object, but as an extension of the consciousness of our myriad different members.

"Finally, know that your perceptions of our Ship may be totally different from anyone else's experience. In fact, because the Ship instantly conforms to your thoughts and needs, YOU will create your own experience of our Mothership. However, because you are still tethered to the many "unconscious" components of your human brain, you may not be fully aware of all your thoughts and emotions.

"Fortunately, once you have integrated your Multidimensional Operating System into your Third Dimensional Operating System, you will no longer be unconscious in any manner. In fact, then you will be able to contain myriad experiences within the NOW," the Arcturian concluded.

I knew better than to ask about these "operating systems," and decided to flow within the NOW. I was rewarded by yet another amazing experience.

"To fully experience your first vision of our

huge Mothership," the Arcturian continued, "turn around inside your mind, and direct your attention into your Core. When you feel your Core around you, look out through your Third Eye while you accept the unconditional love resonating from our Mothership."

I took a long breath to expand my consciousness enough to find my core. Then I turned around inside my mind. I do not know how I did that, but it was an exhilarating experience. Then with my physical eyes closed, I looked out through my Third Eye in the center of my forehead. At first I saw nothing, but gradually the Mothership seemed to move away from its surrounding orbs and move toward me. With great inner discipline, I remained still and focused my intention on feeling unconditional love.

At first the unconditional love that I felt came from the Arcturian next to me. I was familiar with that feeling. Feeling encouraged by the unconditional love emanating from my friend, I directed my attention onto the Mothership. Instantly, I felt an overwhelming feeling of unconditional love, bliss and total euphoria.

In a flash, the Shuttle Craft was in the Docking Bay and the Arcturian was leaving our small craft. I wondered how I got from distant space to being in the Mothership with no elapsing of time. Fortunately, as I asked myself that question, I received the answer. The Mothership resonated beyond time and, hence, beyond space.

The Arcturian ignored my thought process and

quietly waited for me to exit the Shuttlecraft.

Dimensions of the Mothership

MYTRE SPEAKS:

The Arcturian did not want to interfere with my personal perception of the Mothership, so It said nothing as I got my glimpse of the immense Ship. Since the Arcturian Mothership is multidimensional, the Ship has myriad levels. Only those who have calibrated their consciousness to the frequency of each level can perceive that dimension of the Mothership.

If our consciousness is not calibrated to a certain dimension, then that area of the Ship is invisible to us. Fortunately, consciously visiting the Mothership greatly expands our consciousness. Thus, the longer we are on the Ship, the more our consciousness expands into the higher dimensions, and the more of the Mothership we can perceive and visit.

By the time I was invited to visit the Mothership I had recovered the memory of many frequencies of my Multidimensional SELF. However, recovering the memory of a reality is not the same as actually experiencing it. With that said, I will speak of my experiences on the different dimensions of the Mothership.

Third and Fourth Dimensional Sections of the Mothership

There are no third dimensional perceptions of the Mothership, as the Mothership does not exist in that frequency of reality. You may have some perception of the Ship in your fourth dimensional consciousness, but it is actually a memory that has come in through a dream, as the Ship does not exist at that frequency either. I will now go through my dimensional perceptions of the Mothership.

Please remember that these are MY experiences. Another person may perceive the Mothership differently because our attention is drawn to that which is most important in our lives. Therefore, each of us will likely have different experiences, which will depend on our greatest interests. With that said, I will begin.

Fifth Dimensional Sections of the Mothership

At first my fifth dimensional perception was blurry. Fortunately as I relaxed I began to calibrate my attention to the frequency of fifth-dimensional stimuli. The Primary Visitors Center is fifth dimensional. Everyone in this area appears to have a form, but they are not limited to a humanoid body. Since the crew members of this Ship are all fifth dimensional and beyond, they can easily create a humanoid form but often choose to wear their own unique form.

First-time visitors usually go to a Restoration Chamber. However, they will not receive the total treatment that I did unless they are going to remain within the fifth dimension and beyond. It would be too shocking to suddenly get a fifth dimensional body without any instruction about how to use it; and then return to the physical world. On the other hand, many visit the Mothership on a regular basis so that they can gradually adjust to the feeling of a fifth-dimensional body.

From the Visitors Center I was taken to another meeting room where I met with other "trainees" who had been working with different Arcturians. We were each assigned a guide to make sure that our first experience of the Mothership was educational without being overwhelming. We all chatted while we were waiting for our guides and discovered that we had all been trained in the process of creating reality with our thoughts and emotions.

I also discovered that many Earthlings on the Ship were able to harness and use their immense power of emotion because their polarized reality had forced them to "follow their heart." I was not an Earthling. However Pleidians, who are among the primary ancestors of Earthlings, are quite emotional as well.

Just as we trainees were getting to know each other, our guides came into the meeting room and called the name of the trainee they would be guiding. For some reason, my name was called last, which gave me an opportunity to memorize the names of each of my new friends. My guide finally arrived and was an androgynous being wearing a somewhat humanoid form.

As my Guide followed me out of the room, he/she instructed me to follow the *desire* of my emotion. Being able to follow my intuition through the Ship led me to many surprises. For example, I opened a few doors that went nowhere. When I finally asked my Guide about these doors he/she said, "You will have to calibrate to a higher consciousness to perceive beyond these doors. However, we allowed you to open them because it demonstrated that you are not yet ready for those higher frequencies of reality."

Somewhat embarrassed, I quietly closed that door and moved on to open yet another door that led to a frequency beyond my perception. I tried to release my ego and realize that I was gathering important information about myself. However, I judged myself every time I opened a door that I *was not ready* to enter.

I also found that there were many Holosuites on this dimension, mess halls with myriad kinds of nutrition, meeting rooms and viewing rooms. The viewing rooms were my favorite. In these rooms there were huge viewing screens through which we could look outside of the Mothership and see the different stars, constellations and galaxies. I discovered that I was able to use the viewing screen to see whatever area I desired by calibrating my thoughts and emotions to that location.

Furthermore, when I expanded into higher states of consciousness I was able to adjust the viewing screen to perceive higher dimensions of my chosen location. From each perspective of different dimensions I observed entirely different, yet cohesive, versions of the same reality. It was in the Viewing Room that the new visitors practiced their multidimensional perceptions.

With practice, I could later view any area in the galaxy and beyond, by expanding my consciousness into higher and higher frequencies. Of course I wanted to visit my new Homeworld, the Pleiades. However, I think my consciousness was too limited when I thought of my Homeworld as I had too many conflicting emotions about leaving it.

The Bridge

Every dimension of the Mothership has its own dimensional version of the bridge. So as not to interfere with the important business of the bridge, we observed it from a viewing screen. Everyone on the bridge was telepathically connected with the biological mind of the ship. They did not "direct" the ship. It is more appropriate to say that they "consulted" the ship.

The name Mothership is the correct term, as the ship was like a mother to everyone onboard. The ship heard our every thought. In fact, everyone on the Ship heard everyone's thoughts. Interestingly, we heard each other's thoughts in the same manner as you would hear your own thoughts. The differentiation between each person was only in that they wore a form that appeared to be separate.

However, on closer inspection, we could see the

ONE energy field that connected everyone to each other, as well as to the Mothership. The best imagistic language for this scenario is that each being appeared as a separate light on one long cord. The cord connected everyone to each other, as well as to the Ship, and every *light* had is own unique manner of expressing what all the lights were experiencing via the group experience of being connected with the *cord*.

Because the Mothership had so many different beings from so many different worlds, everyone was constantly having the experience of many, many versions of reality. This sensation of being ONE with everyone was the strongest when we tuned into the bridge. In fact, unity consciousness was the fuel that ran the ship. Hence, it was our collective consciousness that kept the Mothership running, while the Mothership simultaneously took care of our every need.

The Mothership is an entire world unto Her SELF. Hence, it is difficult to express what a wonderful experience it was to be at ONE with such a magnificent, living being. We all affectionately called the Mothership "Her." In fact, being on the Mothership is much like being on a planet where all the inhabitants live with full Planetary Consciousness. By "Planetary Consciousness" I mean the ability to tune into and become ONE with every aspect of the planet.

The Illusion of Time

A New Home

I would like to take a moment to divert from my message about the Mothership to talk about the illusion of time. It was aboard the Mothership that I first began to truly understand the NOW. Until I lived on the Mothership, my life appeared to progress in a sequential fashion and the events of each day seemed to progress in a string of perceptions and actions.

However, once I boarded the Arcturian Starship, life no longer appeared sequential. One moment I found myself having an experience in one area of the Ship, and then suddenly I was doing something in a different area. I was very puzzled by this, but when I asked the Arcturian it only said, "You are just addicted to time." I had no idea what that meant, but I was sure I would find out.

Suffice to say, I was still having lessons about *mind over matter*.

Fifth and Sixth Dimensions

MYTRE SPEAKS:

As I slowly adapted to resonating beyond the limitations of time, I could calibrate my fifth dimensional consciousness to any time zone or fifth dimensional area of the Mothership.

Fifth Dimensional Beings on the Mothership

Before I begin our tour of the sixth dimensional sections of the Mothership, I would like to talk about the fifth dimensional Beings onboard the Ship. A fifth dimensional being's form is very mutable, which can easily be altered by their thoughts and emotions.

Therefore, those in fifth dimensional forms may appear to be solid on one occasion, but then suddenly appear in a translucent Lightbody. Lightbody is a very comfortable form as there is very little mass. Lightbodies do not experience bodily sensations such as hunger, thirst, hot or cold. Furthermore, the high frequency of a Lightbody is a wonderful receptacle for unconditional love.

Also, just as a physical being made of the physical elements of its planet "eats" plants and/or animals found on their planet, a Cosmic Lightbody "eats" Cosmic Light. The Lightbody can also instantly receive, maintain, understand and dispense huge amounts of information.

Hence, when a Lightbody is resonating to its highest frequencies, it is a living expression of multidimensional light, as well as that light's highest expression of unconditional love. It is this unconditional love that makes Unity Consciousness such a powerful fuel for our Mothership.

There are areas of the Mothership that are just for visitors. In these areas, everyone chooses to wear humanoid, dense appearing forms to create an easier adjustment for our ascending humanoid friends. Then, when we return to other quarters on the ship, we can feel free to take on whatever form we wish. This process is much like coming home from work and changing into comfortable clothes. However, we change into comfortable bodies.

Within our "comfortable bodies" we can more easily merge with others in the same manner that any light might merge. When we merge our Lightbodies, we instantly experience everything in the same manner as they do. In fact, there are certain occasions when the Mothership and the entire crew merge into the ONE of the NOW.

We find these times to be similar to what some have called heaven. We only create this merging when the visitors are known to be able to accept this intensity of light. As some of you may know, taking on a frequency of light that is too far beyond your base-frequency can cause many issues with your form.

We also experienced this sensation once the

frequency of our Pleiadian world began to expand into the fifth dimension. Hence, we gathered together all the healers and leaders who had already experienced this process and created a network through which the ascending ones could always find help. Establishing this Network was no small task, as most people were already overwhelmed with their own process of ascension.

On the other hand, our network found that when they used the higher frequencies they were downloading that they actually felt better. Light, especially expanding Light, can more easily integrate into any system when it is given a path of movement. Light that is motionless becomes agitated and can create fear and anxiety in the ones who have newly downloaded it.

Sixth Dimensional Sections of the Mothership

I would now like to take you on a tour of the sixth dimensional sections of the Mothership. As I have said before, when I first came to the Mothership, I had expanded my consciousness into my Multidimensional SELF. However, expanding your consciousness into this frequency and actually entering a sixth dimensional reality are not the same experience at all.

Therefore I will take you back to the first door I spoke of, the one that seemed to open to nowhere. This time I will tell you what happened when I finally entered the opened door. I had been on the Mothership for quite a while and had explored much of the fifth dimensional sections of the Mothership.

Hence, I was ready to see more. After a brief hiatus from each other, my Arcturian friend and I had reconnected, and I was continuing my studies. During what I thought was a break from my studies, the Arcturian said, "Let's go back to the door to nowhere."

In a flash of the NOW our fifth dimensional forms were standing in front of that door. I telepathically heard the Arcturian's advice to open it, and so I did. This time was totally different. As soon as the door opened, I was pulled through it and into a world I had never known. I was accustomed to the mutable and sometimes formless fifth dimension, but I was unprepared for the sensations of a six dimensional reality.

I felt as though I was being pulled apart, as if my Lightbody was disarticulating. I could feel fear growing within me, so I centered my attention into the NOW and allowed the unique sensations to take hold of my consciousness. I say "consciousness," for as soon as I went through the door I was completely formless.

I don't know how to say this in a sequential manner, but even my consciousness seemed to be disassociated from any familiar sensations, thoughts, emotions or movements. While in my fifth dimensional Lightbody, I had experienced freedom from my Lightbody by allowing my consciousness to flow beyond what appeared to be the loose form of light that I had called my body.

However, in the sixth dimension my consciousness was dispersed into the totality of this world, and I felt as though my consciousness had been dispersed far into the unknown. Again, I had to deeply connect with the NOW to not allow my energy field to seek my former safety of structure.

I remained focused on NOW, NOW, NOW in order to cling to some center within this field of extremely high energy. Eventually I became aware of what appeared to be patterns within what I had just perceived as nothingness. These patterns were not static, as they fluxed and flowed like a buoy on a stormy ocean.

With that picture in my consciousness, I could see how there was a format, such as the ocean and the air, but they were totally intertwined. It seemed that the "air" created the pattern and the "water" reflected a wavering version of the pattern in the air. Everything was in constant flow. Eventually, as I became accustomed to these sensations, I felt a deep sense of beginnings. I had no idea what was beginning, but the sensation seemed important and felt comforting.

At that moment, the Arcturian also entered the door and touched me on what might have been my Third Eye. Instantly, the room took on a structure. The structure was much like the Viewing Room in the fifth dimension. However, NOW I was viewing, and simultaneously being, the sixth dimension.

"This dimension is a potential reality, which is

infinitely in the process of being formed," I heard the Arcturian tell me. It had informed me before that It spoke telepathically to force me to *abandon my addiction to words.*

"Am I inside the Viewing Screen?" I had to ask.

In response, I was instantly within an experience that I will have to call Creative Potential. I could feel myself dispersing even further and knew I would have to get myself into some degree of form. I had learned that when the Arcturian seemed to abandon me, it was because It knew that I was ready to find the answer within.

I had also learned that if I doubted myself I would never find the solution. Therefore I relaxed into the experience and searched within my inner knowing. The problem was, where was within? I was in a new world now, and all the rules of this reality were unknown to me' except, I still knew that I was a Multidimensional Being.

Consequently, I needed to connect with a sixth dimensional expression of my SELF. I remembered that surrender was the key to all higher dimensional worlds. I surrendered into the experience of floating and flowing in a reality, which I could not see or hear, but could still FEEL. Also, I was able to connect with some sense of my SELF. From within the SELF with whom I was loosely connected, I surrendered completely to that which I could not understand.

As I released the need to understand, a whisper of knowing began to flicker within whatever consciousness I still possessed. The whisper was not in any language, but I felt it as a sensation of *willingness to begin.* I did not know what I was willing to begin, but I chose to surrender to that willingness, as it was the only touchstone I could find.

I allowed the willingness to grow stronger and stronger until it was predominant over the unknown of my experience. Gradually, this willingness became a vague memory that was so dim I could hardly grasp it. Thus, I fell into the memory and embraced it until it took hold of my dispersed consciousness.

Somehow, this distant memory was able to pull me into a very lose form. Suddenly, I was OUT of the "pure potential" and in front of the viewing screen standing/flowing next to the mutable form of the Arcturian.

Can a loose form of Arcturian Light smile? Or, maybe that smile was mine.

The Sixth Dimensional Mothership

MYTRE SPEAKS:

Sixth Dimensional Sections Of The Mothership

As I have said before, every section of the Mothership has its multidimensional components. We have visited the sixth dimensional Viewing Room, which is exactly like the fifth dimensional Viewing Room only it resonates to a higher frequency. When you were in the fifth dimensional version, you could look into the View Screen to see and hear any place in the Universe that you wish to experience.

In the sixth dimensional section, the Viewing Screen is not something that you look through but something that you ARE. There is no sixth dimensional concept for viewing and viewer. Everything is within the Unity Consciousness of the ONE.

Furthermore, the sixth dimension represents the Matrix upon which your creative energies adhere. However, in the sixth dimension you are the Matrix and you are the creative energies. You are the creator of your reality, and through your longing, you prepare the 6D Matrix that will be the foundation of your new reality.

You prepare for your creation by thinking of it

as the wish fulfilled. Then:

- You discipline yourself to perceive peace where there is conflict.
- Discipline yourself to feel love where there is fear.
- Discipline yourself to find unity where there is separation.

In this manner, you create your ascension. **Refuse to linger or put any attention on the components of reality that are ending and focus on the reality that is being born.** Then, gradually, your consciousness begins to disarticulate from the extinct Matrix and sets off in search for a new sixth dimensional Matrix to which you can attach.

The above process is one of the things that I learned by merging with the sixth dimensional Viewing Screen. I visited the sixth dimensional Viewing Screen to learn, practice and master my inter-dimensional travel skills. Inter-dimensional travel is usually done via pure, formless consciousness. I learned that once I attached my consciousness to a given Matrix of reality, I needed to create a form for myself from the energetic molecules of that reality.

The Arcturian told me that I could return to the sixth dimensional Viewing Screens to practice my inter-dimensional travel and creation skills. The molecular patterns of my multidimensional form were safely stored in the sixth dimensional Matrix. Hence, if I wanted to exit a reality or was having difficulty, I could call to the Viewing Screen to bring me back to the Mothership where my base-line cellular form is safely saved.

The Sixth Dimensional Mess Hall

Of course, there is no eating on the sixth dimension, but there is a "filling of our consciousness with the Unity of the Ship." Hence, the area that correlates to the fifth dimensional Mess Hall is a place where we all go to intermingle on a deep, intimate level. I did not realize how sharing a meal was so intimate until I experienced the sharing of energy fields in the sixth dimensional Mess Hall.

Yes, I did become accustomed to this sixth-dimensional frequency of reality, just as all our human expressions are becoming accustomed to the frequency shifts on Ascending Earth. In fact, to better assist our friends and family who have chosen to take a form on Ascending Earth we often invite Gaia, the consciousness of planet Earth, to join us when we blend our energies.

I have found this experience of sharing our energy with Gaia to be very profound. I had never before experienced a planet in such an intimate manner. Gaia is much like any other multidimensional being, except that She has a very large form. One thing that I realized is that every Being on a planet is a component of the macrocosm of that planet.

The humans of Earth have many beings, although they are microscopic, that live on their bodies, just as Gaia has many beings who live on Her planetary body. To Gaia, the form of one human is about as big as one microscopic being that lives on a human's earth vessel. Yet, Gaia keeps guard over all Her inhabitants and is holding back on the completion of Her ascension as long as She can, in hopes that more humans will be able to join Her.

We have been having regular meetings in the Mothership's Mess Hall to assist the humanoids with their ascension process. The rest of Gaia is good to go, but humanoids are the ones having the most difficulty with ascension. We see that many who have chosen to wear the mantle of "power over" have become so lost in that lower expression that they have forgotten their "power within."

In fact, recently we have been focusing on those lost ones to assist them to remember the great inner power to which they have constant access. We are finding that, bit-by-bit, some of them are turning away from that which is ending and towards the hope of a new way of living.

We ask that our ascending ones on Earth join us in assisting the lost ones. If you send them fearful energy, you feed their fear, for ALL bullies are afraid. On the other hand, if you send them loving energies, you feed their hope of awakening. I guess in a way, this Mess Hall is about "feeding," but we feed *others* our love rather than feed *ourselves* food.

Max Is On The Bridge

A New Home

The sixth dimensional Bridge is in correlation with the Fifth Dimensional Bridge, only it resonates to a higher frequency. Since the operating frequency/dimension of the sixth dimensional Bridge is higher, the operating system is quite different. In fact, Max is on the Bridge and is a vital component of the Mothership's Multidimensional Operating System. Actually, the proper way of saying this is that Max is accessible from the Sixth Dimensional Bridge, which resonates beyond all limitation of time or space.

I will give a brief explanation of Max. During Earth's Golden Age, Lemuria and Atlantis used Crystalline Operating Systems to run their societies. These operating systems were in the form of Crystal Skulls. There were once twelve Crystal Skulls, along with Max, who is the thirteenth Crystal Skull. Max contains all the information of the other twelve, as well as much more.

These Crystal Skulls were originally created by the Arcturians and brought to Earth from Arcturus and the Pleiades. First they were given to Lemuria, which was the original of the two societies and based in what is now known as the Pacific Ocean. These Skulls were brought to Earth during the time when a fluid Firmament surrounded Earth. This Firmament protected Earth from hostile invaders, as only unconditional love could penetrate that Firmament.

When the Firmament was in place, Earth was a fully multidimensional world inhabited by androgynous, Spirit Beings. Because of the protective Firmament, Earth resonated to a zero-point, non-magnetic plane with no polarities or illusions. The Beings of early Lemuria and Atlantis knew that their paradise was temporary. Therefore, they inserted holographic records into Max to store the template for their 12-strand DNA, which allowed them to take earth vessels which could house their magnificent multidimensional minds.

The original twelve Crystal Skulls are gone from your reality and Max is in safe keeping in higher dimensional Earth. When Gaia ascends, She will open the files within Max to initiate Her New Earth. Since the Arcturian Mothership resonates beyond time and space, Max is available to our Bridge, as a representative of the full potential of humanity.

Max also serves as the human prototype in the higher dimensions of Earth, where it can be accessed from any reality via the Universal Mind. Any Being who can access the Universal Mind ONLY resonates to the higher frequencies of unconditional love. Therefore, the information is eternally safeguarded from the lost ones who seek "power over" others in the infant societies of the third and fourth dimensions.

The Universal Mind resonates beyond time and space, just like the Mothership. Time and space are aspects of light that resonate to the third/fourth dimension and below. Earthlings are all experiencing great changes in their consciousness and their daily life because time is quickening. Meanwhile, the unconditional love that is embedded in the higher frequency light is flowing into Gaia's world.

Those who have never consciously experienced unconditional love believe that they had to DO something to deserve love. Hence, they desperately do whatever they can in hope that they will be "good enough" to receive love. On the other hand, unconditional love is free; you only need to DO that which fills you with more unconditional love.

It appears I have diverted from Max, but not really, for Max contains the complete, TRUE history of Earth and of Her multidimensional humanity. Therefore, Max represents the perfect prototype of human conscious, as well as all humanity's aspects and potentials. This Mothership is dedicated to the ascension process of planet Earth. In fact the Arcturians and Pleiadians, as well as the Sirians, have been guardians of Gaia from the beginning of Her journey into a polarized reality.

The Arcturians, Pleiadians and the Sirians have worked together to assist Gaia during Her time of great need. The experiment of being a dualistic planet did not go well. Too many great Light Beings became trapped in the 3D Game of separation. We have discovered from Gaia, that Beings cannot be separated from each other and from Source for a very long "time."

Most Light Beings remained connected to each other and to Source for many incarnations.

However, due to the intense fear and lies of a world separated from Source, many became lost in the depths of despair and darkness. Fortunately, the experiment is closing. You now have the option of ascending into Gaia's higher expression of New Earth, where you can join your Multidimensional SELF who awaits your great reunion.

How Max Functions

The crystalline skull known as Max operates via the crystalline power of the fifth dimension and beyond. Max alone would not provide enough energy to command this Mothership. However, the Ship is an alive Being who is allied with the immense Wisdom, Power and Love of the Arcturians, as well as the energy field and the multidimensional consciousness of everyone on our Ship.

Since the Mothership is alive, She makes all necessary decisions in conjunction with the multidimensional mind of all who reside within Her body. As I have said before, we do not tell the Ship what to do. We consult the Mothership regarding the decision that is best for every inhabitant.

It would be impossible to describe the complexity of the Arcturian Group mind, which is primarily responsible for the Mothership. Even I, who am living amongst them, cannot fully understand them. When I first came to the Mothership, I missed my life on the Pleiades. However, that is not a problem any longer for I have expanded my consciousness to the extent that I can consciously visit multiple realities within the now of the ONE.

Soon, dear Earth Family, you will remember your Multidimensional SELF. Then you too will be able to easily expand your conscious awareness beyond your current imaginings.

Suzanne Lie

Sixth Dimensional Beings

MYTRE SPEAKS:

Greetings again! Before we resume our tour of the Mothership I would like to speak more about sixth dimensional Beings. Beyond the fifth dimension, form is a choice which is usually only taken while visiting the denser worlds of the fifth dimension and below. Sixth dimensional Beings on the Mothership seldom choose to wear a form and prefer to live within the Ship's light-network.

In fact, they have much to do with the Ship being alive. Their sixth dimensional energy field is always moving and enlightening the life force of the entire Mothership, as well as all her inhabitants. The sixth dimension of the Mothership is one of the thresholds between portions of the Ship that hold a definitive form, and portions of the Ship that consist of mutable form, or portions which exist as pure consciousness.

The sixth dimensionals are the creators of the wormholes through which the formed and formless Beings can move into and through the various densities of the Mothership. These wormholes are "quite a ride" to experience the first time. Therefore, I will share my first journey through the sixth dimensional wormholes into the higher densities of the Ship.

I had been on the Mothership long enough to have fully acquainted myself with the fifth dimensional areas and was ready not to just visit the sixth dimension, but actually use its quality of infinite movement to activate a wormhole. The Arcturian led me to yet another entrance to seemingly nothing and nowhere. As I entered the "door," I was instructed to release all attachment to my current form. Since this would be my first time through the wormhole, the Arcturian assured me that It would protect my form during my adventure. In fact, the Arcturian chose to accompany me on my maiden voyage.

The lack of form was not as disconcerting this time, as I'd had a while to digest my last sixth dimensional experience. Also, knowing that the flash of light that was guiding me was the Arcturian felt calming and allowed me to stay in the NOW. When I say the *Arcturian Light* was guiding me, you must remember that there is no time or space to separate us. Therefore, it was the knowing of the Arcturian FEEL that was guiding me.

Since there is no time, I cannot say how *long* it took for me to actually look at myself to see to NO me. I was pure consciousness with only a loose, mutable wavering of light. Within this loose image of SELF, I was simultaneously ONE within the Collective Consciousness of the Mothership, which I will describe later. Somehow, I had the capability of mind to think "Wormhole." Before I could complete that thought, a huge wormhole opened before me.

We, the Arcturian's light and my own, were swept into the circular movement of the Wormhole. My consciousness blasted open into an experience, which I could only call euphoria and eternal bliss. "We," as any sense of the concept of "I" was extinct, twisted within these sensations that amplified beyond my ability to put into any sequential format of words.

Unfortunately, or fortunately, because I was loosing all connection to the concept of Mytre, whoever that was, I heard the voice of the Arcturian resonating within my light. Instantly, I fell out of the journey and was back into my familiar form standing just outside of the entrance to the sixth dimension.

"The sixth dimension is the realm of Collective Consciousness in which all life is joined into Oneness," spoke the Arcturian with Its voice, to ground me back into my body. "Your sixth dimensional SELF is a wisp of light seeking a new experience of collective consciousness.

"Once your sixth dimensional light decides to join a reality, it simply inserts itself into the sixth dimensional Matrix for that reality as easily as a third dimensional might slip their hand into a glove. You see, Mytre, the realities of the formless sixth dimensional beings and beyond are much vaster than the realities of form.

"We wish to speak now about why you chose to

take your present form. You came into embodiment because your Soul volunteered to assist your planet, as well as the planet Earth, with their process of transmutation into a higher frequency of reality. We, the Arcturians and Pleiadians, have overseen the long evolution of planet Earth for many millennia.

"Gaia, the collective consciousness of Earth, is preparing to rejoin Her innate state of multidimensional consciousness. Therefore we, as well as many other Pleiadians and Arcturians, have decided to take a human form. To do so, we inserted our sixth dimensional consciousness into the Matrix of Earth during the timeline that would herald the beginning of ascending Earth.

"However, our forms did not stay at the higher frequencies. No, we purposefully delved down through the fifth dimension to connect with our Lightbody, continued down through the fourth dimension to capture our Aura, and we called in all our protection as we bravely traveled through the dark and murky Lower Astral Plane. Finally, our great essence entered the tiny, helpless form of a third dimensional infant.

"Please recognize how much courage and dedication to the Light that it took for us to diminish our great Multidimensional SELF into such a dependent state. If that were not enough, in a very short *time* our human expression forgot our true SELF. Then we only knew of our small, weak physical form. Many more than our hearts could bear to count were lost in the great darkness of the closing cycle of Gaia's plight.

"However, upon our release from our illusionary human form, even those who have become completely embedded in the darkness will eventually return HOME to our true, Multidimensional SELF.

"It is important for our human expressions to remember our true multidimensional nature, as then we/they can:

• Release the illusion of physicality that we have wrapped around our memory
• Release the fear that we had to learn in order to survive our human challenge
• Release the guilt that we were taught
• Release the doubt that clouded our mind
• Release ALL of our memories of darkness, pain, fear and sorrow

"With the release of these third dimensional illusions, our human expressions can more easily find their Way back Home to us, the Higher Expressions of our Multidimensional SELF. It is our duty to inform our human ones that they are always protected. It is also important that we let them know that whatever happens to them within this final leg of their life-long return Home is of no consequence.

"The dense body they are wearing will be transmuted into our true body of LIGHT. However, their Path is not ending. In fact, their Path is moving into a frequency of reality in which the density is not so intense and they will be free of the darkness that has haunted them. We, their Higher Expressions of their human SELF, are leading our brave ones into the Light. We tell you this now Mytre, for soon you will be called upon to directly assist our human expressions on planet Earth."

Suzanne Lie

Consciousness On The Mothership
PART VII

Consciousness and Dimensions

THE ARECTURIAN SPEAKS:

We would like to talk to you about the consciousness of our Mothership. Just as the third/fourth dimensional representations of your SELF are only a small fraction of your Multidimensional SELF, the fifth dimensional representation of our Mothership is only a minute component of our multidimensional Ship. In fact, most of our Mothership exists as pure consciousness, which may or may not choose to take on a form.

Therefore, as we speak about the seventh through twelfth dimensions of the Ship, we must first inform you about the states of consciousness for each dimension. Of course, all of these states of consciousness exist as ONE within the NOW and intertwine in a beautiful, cosmic tapestry of frequency, density, multidimensional light and unconditional love. We will discuss each of these states of consciousness in a sequential manner. But, first we will explain more about the term "state of consciousness."

As you know, you are ALL multidimensional beings who have a huge range of expressions of your complete SELF. These expressions of SELF resonate to a myriad of different yet intermingled realities, planets, galaxies and dimensions. There is NO limit to your wondrous SELF as you move through your involvement within the innumerable realities you have chosen to experience.

Each dimension resonates to a different frequency. Therefore, in order to perceive and interact with any given dimension you must calibrate your thoughts, emotions and form to the resonant frequency of that world. For our purposes, we must add that this definition includes both inner and outer realities, as from the perceptions of your $3^{rd}/4^{th}$ dimensional self there is a separation between the inner and the outer world.

In fact, the concept of separation is one of the primary theses for the third/fourth dimensional "Individual Consciousness." We Arcturians place the third and fourth dimensions within the same reality for they are both ruled by the illusion of time and polarities. We consider the fourth dimensional reality to be the aura and "dream world" of the third dimension.

Every dimension has a correlate state of consciousness to which members of that reality much calibrate their personal consciousness in order to perceive and interact with that world. It is the mastery of that type of consciousness that allows the inter-dimensional traveler to move on to the next dimension and state of consciousness.

- In the third/fourth dimension, one perfects Individual Consciousness.

- In the fifth dimension, one perfects Unity Consciousness.
- In the sixth dimension, one perfects Collective Consciousness.
- In the seventh dimension, one perfects Oversoul Consciousness.

The dimensions beyond the seventh merge into each other, so there is a range of dimensions.

- In the eighth through tenth dimensions, one perfects Ascended Master and Elohim Consciousness.
- In the eleventh through twelfth dimensions, one perfects Angelic and Source Consciousness."

There are many pros and cons of Individual Consciousness. Many members of the third dimension find great difficulty in finding the pros for that dimension because they are too shrouded in fear. On the other hand, many members of the third dimension are quite happy. However, their happiness is usually because they have connected with their Multidimensional SELF.

From our perspective in the eighth through tenth dimensions the experiment of Individual Consciousness has been a rousing success. Yes, it is a harsh world in which one either "makes it" or dies trying. And many, many third-dimensionals have died trying to master the very challenging state of consciousness in which they are totally separated, not only from each other, but also from the very God that they have been told to worship.

While one's consciousness is constrained to Individual Consciousness, they can become so self-absorbed that they forget that the energy they put out will come back to them. Hence, many evil deeds have flourished in third dimensional worlds. On the other hand, those who are able to reach inside their "individual" self discovered that they felt much better if they loved rather than feared. These awakening ones learned that if they made others feel better, it made them feel better too.

And then there are the many "lost ones" who have completely forgotten their Multidimensional SELF. Therefore, they cannot reach inside themselves to feel the Power-Within and believe they must live their life in a Power-Over-Others manner. Some of these lost ones have lived so many lives in the pursuit of selfish gain that they have totally forgotten the Law of Return because they have never given. They have only taken from others—again and again.

Since they felt separate from the ones from whom they took, they did not realize how the constant taking without any balance of giving was harming their heart. The physical heart is a very special organ. It appears to be a simple pump that moves the blood throughout your system.

However, the heart is also attached to the Thymus Glands of the immune system. All the ductless/endocrine glands, such as the Thymus, are the portions of the physical body that are connected to and driven by Spirit. A heart that is simply a pump and not a portal for the Spirit is a heart that will run low on fuel and need to take fuel from others. It is this concept that the most lost of the "individual ones" have used for their own selfish gains.

We choose not to go into the details of this action except to say that the darkness of Individual Consciousness is the reason why we have to shut down this 3D Game. Also, cosmically, the 3D Game is due to advance into the higher frequencies at this current NOW of planet Earth. It is largely because of the above-alluded intensions of the lost ones that we Arcturians have been allowed to intercede on behalf of Gaia, the consciousness of Earth.

We, and other members of Gaia's Cosmic Family, have decided that Individual Consciousness cannot be allowed to run unchecked. The ceiling can be very high, and many humans have achieved grand feats and ascended into the higher realms of life. However, the underbelly of this state of consciousness cannot be allowed to continue. Power-Over-Others and Service-To-Self was first introduced into your DNA by the Lizzies and Dracs, who ran their world in an "eat or be eaten" predatory manner.

However, the Adam Kadmon body (prototype for humanity's human form) was too delicate to support this Service-To-SELF DNA without damaging the neural pathways that allowed for advancing into higher states of consciousness. Furthermore, the Kundalini Energy that allowed this body type to assist in evolution could turn immensely vicious and cruel if that energy found itself going *down* the spinal cord instead of *up* the spinal cord. We, the creators of humanity's Adam Kadmon prototype, apologize for this defect.

There is no excuse for that mistake, and our only regret is that we did not first research more effectively the possibility that such a deep corruption could enter that frequency of reality. The overall effect has been that the extreme polarities of an angelic body format intermingled with Draconian DNA. This intermingling did create world saviors with more courage and fortitude than imaginable to the members of a world that had not known polarity for millions of your years.

Unfortunately, the negative result was just as extreme. Those who were lost to the darkness passed into the Lower Astral Realm to haunt and torment those who wished to advance their consciousness beyond the limits of strict, third dimensional thinking.

The few who achieved Mastery set up Mystery Schools just past the dark world of the Lower Astral to rescue the brave ones who could find their way through that abyss of darkness. They then began forming the structure of Mystery Schools at the Threshold of each of the sub-planes of the fourth dimension. In this manner, we could better assist the ones who were attempting to move beyond the strict confines of the Individual Consciousness.

The problem with Beings of Light is that we sometimes underestimate predatory Beings who wish to harm and control. We have learned much about courage from the third dimensionals; these brave members of the Adam Kadmon family who have had to confront the many limitations of the third dimensional reality.

Despite the predatory nature that lurked within their DNA they faced the constant threat of disaster, defeat, disease and death and still advanced their consciousness into the realm of Personal and Planetary Ascension. We stand in awe of their accomplishments and salute their ability to embrace the unconditional love in the midst of their many challenges.

Unity and Collective Consciousness

THE ARCTURIAN SPEAKS:

Fifth Dimensional Unity Consciousness

Individual consciousness is a microcosmic version of reality in which the least evolved humans perceive themselves as a separate, individual physical body. On the other hand, the most evolved human perceives his or herself as a member of the entire planet. At the lowest stage of evolution, the human has Individual Consciousness, which gradually encompasses more and more elements of reality until he or she has come into a consciousness of Unity With ALL planetary life.

When your Unity Consciousness includes the planet, the format for personal and planetary ascension has been laid. Once you have progressed from perceiving yourself as one human, to being an entire planet, you are ready to expand your sense of SELF beyond your planet and into the Galaxy.

When the solar and galactic energies are powerful enough to ascend a planet, there is an option for planetary ascension as well as personal ascension. In fact, during the current energy field of your reality there is an option for ascension into the next octave of reality for your entire local universe.

Earth has suffered extremes of polarity, but now

She has the greatest potential for entrance into higher octaves of expression. Furthermore, we the former residents of Earth are combining our higher frequencies of consciousness with that of Gaia. It is the least we can do to assist Gaia who has offered Her body as a schoolroom for so many of our galactic family members.

In fact, a primary manner in which you, the ascending humans of Earth can assist the ascension of Gaia is to join into Unity Consciousness with your Galactic Family in the fifth dimension and beyond. Once you have done so, you will gain immediate access to your Multidimensional SELF.

With the continual awareness of your Multidimensional SELF any remaining polarities of Earth will disappear along with the other third dimensional illusions. With illusion released from your consciousness, your reason for a separate form is easily erased.

We the members of your Galactic Family, who are also members of your Multidimensional SELF, are amazed at how much one human can accomplish alone. Hence, we have total confidence that your unity with Gaia will be more than sufficient to ride the powerful energy field shift into Gaia's fifth dimensional SELF. The more humans who can simultaneously shift into the fifth dimensional Unity Consciousness with Gaia, the easier the "ride" will be.

We shall now focus only on the consciousness of the Mothership. The fifth dimensional Unity

Consciousness of the Ship is easily augmented by the sixth dimensional, Collective Consciousness of the Ship.

Sixth dimensional Collective Consciousness

We say *OF the ship* rather than *ON the ship* for the Mothership is an alive Being. In order to enter the sixth dimensional areas of the Mothership, you must be able to experience and feel comfortable within a sixth dimensional state of Collective Consciousness. Sixth dimensional, Collective Consciousness is not the same as fifth dimensional, Unity Consciousness.

The beings of fifth dimensional Unity Consciousness appear to be wearing separate forms and/or forms that are connected by the visible surrounding ethers. On the other hand, sixth dimensional beings usually prefer a formless state. However, they are willing to wear a form if called upon to do so. When they do take a body, it is usually quite beautiful as they are the "matrix makers" and enjoy creating loving and beautiful representatives of their Essence.

If necessary, sixth dimensional beings will create temporary forms while engaged in a group commitment. However, outside of *time*, the term *temporary* has a different meaning. There are two types of form that sixth dimensionals take:

• One of these is the form of a matrix, which serves as the foundation for any given construct such as a planet or the Mothership.

• The other form is an entity of Collective Consciousness that appears as one great Cosmic Being.

These life forms are usually so large that they can only live in Outer Space. In both of these cases, *temporary* means that their form will continue to evolve and shift.

Multidimensional Perceptions

Many of you, our ascending ones, have remembered how to simultaneously perceive more than one dimension. For example, more and more of you simultaneously perceive both the third and fourth dimensions. You are called "psychic" because you have access to the fourth dimensional world while in your waking life. Most of you also have Lucid Dreaming while asleep. Hence, you can intermingle the two worlds.

As you remember to maintain a steady connection to the fifth dimension while still wearing your earth vessel, you will be able to simultaneously perceive three worlds:

• Your physical world

• Your fourth dimensional world that exists within your aura and

• Your fifth dimensional world of New Earth

Just as you close your eyes to better perceive your fourth dimensional dreams during sleep, you will be able to focus only on the fifth dimension by closing your eyes to the lower density worlds. Once in the fifth dimension, you can also keep a consciousness portal open to the third/fourth dimensions in case your services are needed there.

This multidimensional process is much like voicemail on your telephone, or even the ring of the phone. However, this inter-dimensional *phone* is not an external device, but an internal monitor of your entire multidimensional reality. Until all the third/fourth dimensions of Gaia are closed, you will likely constantly monitor what is remaining of the Shadow of Gaia in the lower dimensions to see if your assistance is needed.

Many of you who are actively involved in the ascension process of Gaia will serve as Greeters on New Earth. You will all have the ability to either "take a vacation" from this role, or to simultaneously experience the higher realms of the fifth dimensional Gaia while also serving as a Greeter. In fact, once you have released the anchor of your third/fourth dimensional self, you will be able to carry more than one reality within your aware consciousness at all times.

Comparing Unity and Collective Consciousness

Your fifth dimensional Unity Consciousness is based on the multidimensional unity of both the lower and higher frequencies of reality. Once you include your sixth dimensional Collective Consciousness into your multidimensional awareness, there will be a vast shift in how you perceive reality. The beings of the fifth dimension are usually still enjoying the experience of creating form. Hence, the spectrum of the first dimension through the fifth dimensions of consciousness is inhabited by beings that usually maintain an individual or group form.

Therefore, within Unity Consciousness myriad forms interact in unconditional love and acceptance. Many fifth dimensionals enjoy shifting from form to form, or consciously maintaining many forms at a time. Conversely, the beings of the sixth dimension enjoy the experience of creating the matrix upon which a form can be maintained, while they still exist as formless beings of light.

Islands of Light

At first the New Earth, which is on the threshold of the fifth dimension, will appear much like your present Earth. However, on New Earth there will be only love, only unity and only peace. In fact, it may feel like you are having a wonderful dream where you can create everything with your thoughts and emotions.

The reality is that many of you already live predominantly in New Earth and interface with the third/fourth dimensional Earth when you "go to work." Furthermore, some of you even enjoy fifth dimensional work. From our perspective, we see many Islands of Light that have been created by our ascending ones.

We observe how many of you ascending ones

move your consciousness in and out of these Islands by either maintaining Mastery over your energy field or by temporarily losing control of your energy field and falling out of frequency range to New Earth. Once you fall out of the resonance of New Earth, you return to the third/fourth version of Earth.

All reality is based on stages and degrees. You may have 10% of your consciousness calibrated to the fifth dimensional expression of Earth. Then you may meditate or do something that you love and suddenly you are 80% calibrated to the fifth dimension. In the higher densities all life is intermingled like drops of water in the ocean.

Therefore, you do not leave one reality and then enter another. You have a certain percentage of your being within several dimensions within the Now of the ONE. The reality to which the greatest percentage of your consciousness is focused is experienced as your primary reality. Then, just as you can talk to a friend on the phone, make dinner, talk to your children and jot a note at the "same time," you can live many realities within the NOW of the ONE.

All of these realities of form will be experienced at once via your fifth dimensional Unity Consciousness. Also, the fifth dimensional reality is NOT separate form the third/fourth, as the fifth dimension connects you to your Multidimensional SELF. Within each dimension, reality displays the same "story line," but from a different frequency of reality.

In contrast to Unity Consciousness in which *separate* beings gather to create a united reality, the sixth dimensionals have NO concept of separation. Their formless state *collects* in order to create the matrix/foundation for a reality. These realities are "fleshed out" by the beings of the fifth dimension.

Remember, ALL of you are multidimensional. Therefore, ALL of you exist in ALL dimensions simultaneously. However, you are not aware of these realities unless your consciousness is calibrated to that world. Furthermore, the higher dimensions can easily perceive the lower dimensions, but the lower dimensions cannot perceive the higher ones.

In order to perceive the higher dimensions, you have to expand your consciousness into the frequency of that reality. Then your consciousness serves as a frequency telescope. Once you calibrate your telescope toward the frequency of a given reality, you can perceive that reality.

Inter-dimensional Memories

However, perceiving and interacting with a reality is not the same. You can passively "look into" a higher dimensional reality while maintaining a lower dimensional form. Conversely, in order to interact with that reality, your entire Essence must be calibrated to the frequency of that reality.

To calibrate your entire form, you will need to release your attachment to your other expressions of

SELF and know that your Multidimensional SELF is the storehouse for all your genetic coding and frequency patterns. Then, using the power of your unconditional love, you can open the portal to a reality and create a form from the elements of that reality.

Moving into a reality that is free of form after such a long sojourn into the physical world is an experience that is best delayed until you have fully remembered your inter-dimensional skills. For some of you, the memory of being formless will instantly pass into your consciousness because you have been remembering them while still holding a form. For others, who have long been disconnected from their multidimensional nature, it will be best to recover from your physical amnesia of your SELF before you venture into formless worlds.

We shall return to discuss an introduction to the seventh dimension, Oversoul Consciousness, as well as the seventh dimensional area of the Mothership.

Nightly Visits

THE ARCTURIAN CONTINUES:

Dear Ascending Ones, many of you visited our Starship last night because important decisions were being made, and we wanted to confer with our Ground Crew. You may have remembered the experience if you woke up in the middle of the night or in the morning, but forgot it as you went about your day.

Because of past traumas, and/or because it is difficult to stay grounded when you remember the myriad activities of your Multidimensional SELF, you may have difficulty clearly remembering your nightly visits to our Ship. However, many of your past traumas have been healed, and you have improved your grounding abilities and expanded your consciousness.

Therefore, you are ready to begin the process of regaining your multidimensional memory. Once you fully regain this memory you will be able to live in more than one reality at a time. Many of you have always done so in your imagination, but now you are ready to progress into the next phase in which you can simultaneously remember your galactic realities and human reality.

To stimulate your multidimensional memory, we will review our latest meeting with our Ground

Crew. Thus, please allow yourself to access any dream memories of last night. You may vaguely remember being in a meeting about the landings. We do not choose to discuss the process of disclosure, for we know that no one is ready to take on this responsibility. However, the time of waiting is coming to an end, and humanity must prepare for their return to a Galactic Society, which they were before the fall of Atlantis.

Humanity's planetary evolution was greatly set back by the low frequency of Earth after the fall of Atlantis. However, it is the NOW for those who are on the Path of Ascension to accept the assistance that we wish to give them. Many of the humans in power will not surrender their power-over-others, and too many still slumber in third dimensional consciousness to realize the urgency of this moment.

Hence, countless humans are still trapped in the rules and regulations of the third dimensional world. Some humans cannot release their attachment to the material world and others are too downtrodden to look up into the skies to even see our Ships. Consequently, we will need to bring our Scout Ships closer to the Earth. The meeting you attended was about us considering the best manner in which to land while causing the least amount of fear and confusion.

As you are aware, we have increased our meetings with influential members of your planet. We have also been uncloaking ourselves everywhere, as that which is familiar is not as frightening. However, many humans are so frightened by the many challenges of third dimensional life, and so brainwashed by the mainstream news, that they cannot tolerate anything new entering their consciousness.

We realize that many of these people will not choose ascension, for they are far from gaining mastery of even the third dimension. Because of the above reasons, we have decided to begin our landings in a frequency range just beyond the third dimensional resonance.

This dimensional landing is actually much better for us, as our Scout Ships resonate to the upper fourth and fifth dimensions. Therefore, if we land just beyond the fourth dimensional overlay of the physical plane, often known as the etheric plane, only those who have expanded their consciousness will be able to perceive us.

In this manner, those of you who are suffering doubt, thinking that you have been "crazy" or "wrong" in your belief in our Landings, will gain much-needed assurance. Conversely, those who are deeply enmeshed in the toils of the third dimensional world will not even perceive us. Landing our Scout Ships in a slightly higher frequency than your daily life has another benefit, as it initiates the activation of your expanded perceptions.

Ascension is the process of recalibrating your consciousness to perceive the reality that is resonating to a higher frequency than that physical world. Imagine you are an Avatar logged into a video game with consciousness, self-awareness. In fact you are, as Earth at this frequency is a holographic projection. Since you are a projection from your Multidimensional SELF who decided to copy and paste its consciousness into the 3D Game, you can ask your SELF to assist you to logout of the Game. On the other hand, you will assist your higher dimensional SELF by attaching your awareness to higher and higher frequencies of the Game.

You will accomplish this task by expanding your attention and intention into the parts of your current reality that you love. At the same time, you will release ALL attachments to that which is fearful, distracting and/or no longer important. In other words, you will become the Master of your Energy in that you choose NOT to engage in that which you no longer wish to experience.

This letting go is much like crossing the "monkey bars" of your childhood. Monkey bars are a horizontal ladder above you that are attached to two vertical bars. As an adult, you can easily stand on the ground and touch the horizontal ladder, but when you were a child, the ground was far beneath you. This analogy is perfect for your current situation.

To proceed with your process of letting go of the old and attaching to the new is similar to crossing the monkey bars when one hand was attached to the ladder, while the other hand was in the air, ready to reach for the next rung of the ladder. In this manner, you are ascending by removing your attention from that which you no longer wish to experience and reaching out with your consciousness to grasp that which you know is of a higher frequency.

You know it is a higher frequency because you can feel the unconditional love. Whenever you allow yourself to FEEL this unconditional love, your consciousness will expand. This expanded consciousness will make it simple for you to release your third dimensional worries and illusions. Then, with the release of these worries from your mind you'll be able to FEEL more of the unconditional love that has been *calling* you for years.

You have ignored this *call* too often; for you thought it was not real. We tell you NOW that your third dimensional fears and worries are NOT REAL! Only the higher light of unconditional love, and all that unconditional love creates, is REAL. We are asking you to shift your focus away from your worries of physical life and into the fifth dimension and beyond.

We suggest that you take baby steps so that you can totally ground yourself to each octave of Gaia's ascending planet. If you are having doubt, follow the animals and the children. They have not been tainted by the power-over-others system of your world governments. They do not believe that they have to DO something to be "good enough" and still hold the innocence and purity of being connected to the land and the ONE.

Therefore, we recommend that you release your attachment to the myriad years of indoctrination that you have received at the close of the Kali Yuga. We suggest that you return to the pure innocence of your inner, Divine Child and take the risk to LET GO of your attachment to that which drags your consciousness into fear, anger and/or sorrow. These fear-based emotions attach you to the 3D Matrix.

On the other hand, you can still pay your bills, go to work and put gas in your automobile while knowing that NONE of these actions are real. ALL of these actions are illusions of the third dimensional paradigm. Hence, you will do these actions with NO attachment or emotion. The play is over, and you are leaving the theater. You are just taking a moment of your "time" to pick up your program, push up your seat, and stand in line to leave the theater. The theater is not disappearing yet. In fact, many people are still staring at the empty stage, as if they are waiting for one more act to commence.

If you wish, you can tell them that the play is over. However, most of them will not hear you and may even become angry that you are telling them what they do not want to hear. They are used to this play. They don't want this play to end. They did not understand this play and need to watch more of it in order to know why they even entered this theater in the first place. Therefore, you politely step past them, maybe send them some unconditional love as you leave the theater, and step out into the light of that which awaits you.

Those who are not ready for this new light will remain in a version of the "theater" that is calibrated to their state of consciousness. On the other hand, YOU—the ones who choose to face the unknown, will meet the adventure for which your heart has always longed. We know that you have heard many promises and been disappointed when they did not come to pass. But have you not noticed how much your world has changed?

Remember your life just eleven years ago. Go back in your memory just eleven years. It was October of 2002. What was the state of your world then? It was less than one year after the debacle of 9-11. How many lies were being disseminated and largely believed, in spite of vast evidence to the contrary? How many people had died a violent death and continued dying in many wars that arose from that day? What do you think the primary emotion was on that the planet at that time? Do you think it was fear? If so, you are totally correct.

Now look at the predominant state of consciousness on Earth NOW. In spite of all that you may be seeing, we see that the primary emotion on Earth NOW is Love and Hope! In only ten years, you — our brave grounded ones — have once again brought Gaia from the threshold of total destruction. How did you do that?

In fact, we ask each and every one of you to go

inside and remember how you found a way to rise above the immense fear and wars to somehow change from fear, anger and sorrow into the growing world-wide love and hope. We say to YOU personally, "YOU are a miracle!!"

You could have chosen to attach your consciousness to a reality based on revenge, war, fear and domination. However, instead you have chosen to resonate to another reality. You are living a reality in which a critical component of the world population, which includes plants, animals and Gaia Herself, is preparing and/or is fully prepared for the transition into New Earth.

Do you know how short only 10 years is in Cosmic Time? How long does it take a 3D planet to form? How long does it take a 3D planet to be ready to support life? How long has Earth been created? How long ago did the dinosaurs roam Her land and fly in Her sky? Now think, how long is ten years? How much have you changed yourself in the last ten years?

How much have you changed your thinking, your mastery of emotions and your state of consciousness in JUST 10 years? Do you see now why we call you a Miracle? Yes, we have helped you, but we ARE you! We, your Galactic and Celestial Family are higher frequency expressions of your Multidimensional SELF. If we are you and we are helping you, then YOU are helping yourself.

Therefore, take credit for the great Wisdom you have gathered, the immense Power you have displayed and the beautiful Love that you have shared with every member of Gaia's planetary world. When you go back into your past only ten years, you can see how time is beginning to collapse. To accomplish such an expansion of consciousness in such a short time is impossible for a reality founded on time.

However, time and the slow spin of polarities that time has created is ending. Time is an expression of the resonant frequency of the planet. As Earth is resonating to higher and higher frequencies, polarities are collapsing into the ONE and time is collapsing into the NOW. You, our grounded ones, are greatly facilitating this process by expanding your states of consciousness.

It is for this reason, as well as because of the great courage of the Beings, human and non-human, that so much has changed so vastly in such a short amount of time. This closing of polarities and termination of time is exponentially accelerating. Therefore, hold on to your hope and unconditional love, as you listen to us — your SELF!

Suzanne Lie

The Mothership's Expanded Consciousness

PART VIII

More about Consciousness on the Mothership

THE ARCTURIANS BEGIN:

Our dear ascending ones, we will give you a brief introduction into the Loop of Consciousness that travels between the Seventh Dimensional Oversoul and your Super-subconscious mind. Your Oversoul contains information and pattern codes for every expression of form that you have carried in all your incarnations within the Milky Way Galaxy. This means, every incarnation you have ever had on any planet or dimension within your current galaxy.

On the other hand, your Super-subconscious contains information and pattern codes for every incarnation you have had on the planet Earth, in whatever form that was. Therefore, your Super-subconscious also tells you of your human and non-humanoid forms. In fact, both your Oversoul and your Super-subconscious contain information about all the types of form you have chosen to experience.

Your Super-subconscious is limited to all your incarnations on Earth, but your Oversoul has no restrictions at all as it resonates far beyond the frequencies of any concept of limitation. The loop that we speak of is the connection between these two frequencies of consciousness as related to your personal choices of form, your Super-subconscious, and your galactic choices of form, your seventh dimensional Oversoul.

We have found that the most effective introduction for any given state of consciousness is to have Mytre share his first conscious experience. We say "conscious" for these states of consciousness exist always, whether or not you are aware of them. Also, your Multidimensional SELF is infinitely aware of you, all your expressions of SELF from your Super-subconscious to your Oversoul. As you continue your ascension process, you will be ready and able to access information within your own Multidimensional SELF that you never knew existed.

It is this level of awakening and awareness that is necessary to fully assist with planetary ascension. Remember, you are the planet and the planet is you. You represent a creature of Her world. Whenever you clear yourself, you clear Gaia. As you ascend, you will become aware of the many forms within the NOW of Gaia's ONE.

MYTRE SPEAKS:

Greetings again. It is wonderful to connect with all of you within our Unity and Collective Consciousness. As a Pleiadian, I was aware of alternate and parallel realities. However, before our ascension I never considered that there were so many different expressions of my life force in so many different forms. I will explain this statement by sharing my first experience of the Super-subconscious.

During my initiation in the wilderness of our new Pleiadian home, which I shared with Mytria, I had my first experience with the Super-subconscious. It was then that I learned to communicate directly with the planet. In fact, personal communication with your planet is one of the primary ways in which you, our Earth Friends, can assist your planetary and personal ascension.

When I began to study with the Arcturian aboard the Starship, I was called upon to move deeply into my subconscious in order to gain full mastery of my thoughts. It was then that I first became aware of the myriad talents hidden in my Super-subconscious brain. As a pilot of Starships, I thought of the Super-subconscious as the "engine room" of my brain. If I wanted to boost the functioning of my daily life, I would need to go into the *engine room* of my brain and start up any unused power supplies.

These power supplies where the vast reservoirs of forgotten information from my past/alternate/parallel realities as a Pleiadian. It took extensive training in what you call meditation for me to access this area of my brain. I am not talking about my mind, as our brains live in our bodies and our bodies resonate within our "mind-field."

At the culmination of each life, all the information gained within that life is stored in your Super-subconscious. This information is limited to your Homeworld, or actually the body type of our Homeworld, as different forms on different worlds have different types of realities. Once we move beyond the confines of our planet, we keep this information stored in our deep subconscious to be brought to the surface when we are ready to transmute into Lightbody.

The Super-subconscious is the "computer file" that collects all the necessary information that you have gained on all of your incarnations on your planet, so that you can assist that planet with its ascension into the higher expression of becoming a Galactic Being. Being a Galactic Society does not necessarily mean planetary ascension, as it does in your current society. Actually, what is occurring on Earth is a very unique situation. However, the transition of the humanity's collective consciousness from a planetary reality to a galactic reality represents a huge paradigm shift.

Fortunately, all the information that has ever been gained in any planetary incarnation is stored in the Sub-superconscious. The Super-subconscious is very primal, yet exceedingly advanced. In other words, this consciousness carries all the information regarding your evolutionary process from your most primal self into the state of consciousness in which you are ready to expand beyond the physical world, into the fifth dimension and beyond.

However, I remind you that you are a Multidimensional Being. Therefore, there are many versions of YOU running within myriad dimensions, galaxies and planets. Your Super-subconscious is the holder for each particular world, whereas your Oversoul carries the information regarding ALL the realities of your Galactic Self.

I will begin with sharing the opening of my personal, Pleiadian file.

When the Arcturian came to me and told me that I was ready to view my Super-subconscious, I had no idea what it was talking about. Since I trusted the Arcturian completely, I followed it into our well-used Holosuite. I was led into the dimly lit room and was asked to close my eyes and go into a deep state of meditation. Due to my training I was able to easily move into that state of consciousness.

I then felt the Arcturian touch the back of my head, just above the top of my neck area. Instantly a myriad of pictures, thoughts, emotions and memories coursed through my thoughts in a swirling pattern of disorderly order. I wanted to attach my attention to one sensation, but I was becoming exceedingly dizzy.

My bodily sensations became confused, as did my orientation in space. I did not know if I was standing, sitting, being still or moving around the room. It seemed that I was doing all of the above simultaneously. Besides that I began to see, hear, smell and feel images, memories and sensations.

I was wondering how all this information could be of any use when it was presented in such a confusing fashion. Thus, I tried to push the information away, which only seemed to amplify it.

That is when I heard the Arcturian say, "Move into your animal self." I had no idea what it meant, but then I understood completely after it touched me again in that same area.

Suddenly, the stimuli were understandable. On the other hand, "understandable" is an incorrect term, as it is a humanoid term. When I was "in my animal," I did not need to understand because I could *accept*. I did not accept it because I knew it; I accepted it because it WAS.

Inside my mind, I was calmly viewing a vast collage of differing experiences, sensations and memories. "Open your Eyes," I heard the Arcturian say, but it was said without words. It was a telepathic message that seemed familiar and comfortable. When I opened my eyes, I saw around me what I had seen inside of my head, imagination, Super-subconscious.

I was experiencing the same images inside me, as were around me. They all overlapped, flowed and joined into Oneness, while each image also stood alone. As I looked through my eyes, I began to become overwhelmed and totally confused.

"Return to your animal," I telepathically heard the Arcturian. It took great effort to disengage my humanoid brain, but the Arcturian was not going to assist me this time. I was on my own and had to figure out how to BE the animal that did not question - instead of the human who lived in doubt. The dizziness was becoming intolerable and my nausea was mounting.

A New Home

I was on the verge of passing out when I realized that I was holding my breath. Why was I so afraid? The dizziness was returning, and I was beginning to feel nauseated again. I was a warrior. As I focused my thoughts on my self, I began to breathe. However, I was also losing touch with my animal self, as well as all that information. The word arrogance came into my mind. Of course, I was so much better than an animal, which was a way of ignoring that I was living inside an animal body.

When I realized what I was doing I began to identify, not with my human self, but with my animal self that provided my consciousness a form. Somewhere in my series of incarnations I had developed a sense of superiority over the very form that allowed me to visit the third/fourth dimension. No wonder I was dizzy. I was disconnected from the portion of my being that created a form through which I could experience this reality. I "heard" a smile from the Arcturian. Is it possible to hear a smile? Well, if I could perceive every animal form I had every inhabited, and there were many, I guess anything is possible.

As I settled into my animal nature, I began to understand the images around me in the Holosuite and inside my mind. I could not begin to translate my understanding into a human language. Nonetheless, certain locks seemed to open in my brain.

The key to opening these locks was to release

my attachment to the arrogance and sense of superiority of my humanoid nature, and BE my animal.

Mytre

The Seventh Dimension of the Mothership

THE ARCTURIANS SPEAK:

Mytre has shared his experience of his Super-subconscious being. We will now tell you about the Super-subconscious of our Mothership. Of course, all states of consciousness intermingle within the Being of our Mothership, but just as your brain has certain areas that are more inclined to generate certain states of consciousness, our Ship has certain areas that generate certain frequencies of emanation which encourage correlated states of consciousness.

The Super-subconscious, which represents your animal container, represents the *container* of our Ship. In other words, the Super-subconscious of the Mothership is responsible for all the maintenance of the ever-changing form of the Ship. Just as your animal body grows and changes in reaction to different energy fields; our Mothership's living structure constantly changes according to different situations.

All information of all interactions and alterations of the Mothership since her multidimensional manifestation are stored in the Ship's Super-subconscious. The Mothership that we have been discussing is actually a prototype, an archetypical example of most of our Motherships. Because this Ship has the most extensive Log of interactions with ascending realities, we have chosen Her to assist Gaia with Her Planetary Ascension.

We, the Arcturians, have no aging process, as we do not exist within time. Furthermore, we prefer to visit or use form rather than wear it. We think of form as you might think of a coat. You would not wear a coat unless it was necessary. Furthermore, while you are in the privacy of your home, you wear clothing that is comfortable. However, if guests come to visit, you may put on a special outfit.

In the same manner, while we are relaxing on the Ship, we are usually formless. However, we put on the appropriate form when we have visitors. The *appropriate form* is the version of our vaguely humanoid body that is most pleasing and comfortable to our guests. Hence, we usually wear a form with a head, body, two arms and two legs. On the other hand, when we have non-humanoid visitors, we often adapt our form to be similar to theirs.

Our Mothership can change shapes, and any shape that the Mothership has ever adapted is stored in Her Super-subconscious which is generally located, but not limited to, the bottom areas of the Ship. We are aware that you are accustomed to thinking in terms of top and bottom. Hence, we will use them.

However, there are many occasions in which our Mothership takes on the form of an orb, and there is no bottom or top. In this case, your human thinking would conceive that the Super-subconscious is on the outside of the Ship. These assumptions are also incorrect, as outside and inside are human terms that do not apply to our reality.

We are happy to speak in terms in which you can create a mental picture. On the other hand, please realize that your sequential manner of thinking will greatly limit your ability to understand the fifth dimension and beyond. We are pleased to see that many of you are attempting to adapt to your innate, multidimensional thinking.

Just as our Super-subconscious carries the patterns of every form the Ship has ever taken, our Seventh Dimensional consciousness holds the patterns of every Oversoul of every reality with whom we have interfaced. Allow us to define Oversoul for you. The seventh dimension is the last dimension that engages form as a means of expression.

Beings of the eighth dimension and beyond, such as the Arcturians, lower their resonance into their seventh dimensional Oversoul and *go through that closet* to find every form they have ever worn in any reality. Of course, this is a metaphoric definition, but if we were to speak in our timeless, formless Light Language, you would not understand us.

Therefore, we must search the information in

the brain of our embodied representative to translate our message. Our language is imagistic and is best translated in a metaphoric manner. However, these metaphors would not be technologically correct. Also, know that technology and creativity are the same term in our reality. With that explanation, we will say that the Oversoul is the Soul of the Soul.

From the "bottom" of the pyramid of incarnation into the physical, individuals merge into increasingly expanded perceptions of their SELF as their consciousness expands. For example, the base of the pyramid would be the Individual/Personal experience of SELF. Over 3D time, this experience of SELF expands into a Familial/Cultural experience of SELF, then into a National expression, than to a Planetary expression of SELF.

You, our ascending ones, have fully embraced your Planetary SELF and are preparing to perceive yourselves as your Galactic SELF. You have completed your cycle of polarized individuality and are ready to enter the fifth dimensional expression of your Galactic SELF.

There are Galactic Beings who are not yet fifth dimensional, and you can enjoy that experience, as well. Your Galactic expression of SELF will eventually expand into your Universal expression of SELF.

Please remember that your Multidimensional SELF is infinitely alive and aware. Therefore, when we speak of your progression, we actually mean *the progression of the primary focus of the consciousness of expression of your SELF* to whom we are speaking. However, ALL of your expressions are simultaneously expanding into higher frequencies of reality or diminishing into lower frequency expressions of SELF, such as taking a new physical form.

Hence, as your individual focus of SELF expands into your Planetary SELF, your Planetary focus of consciousness expands into your Galactic SELF and your Galactic focus expands into your Universal SELF. Your higher dimensional expanded SELF can easily perceive and interact with your lower dimensional versions of SELF.

Therefore, you will not necessarily lose contact with your Personal expression of SELF when Gaia ascends. However, just as you can see a rock, but the rock does not see you, your lower dimensional expressions of SELF can only communicate with their higher expressions by expanding their consciousness to encompass that frequency of reality.

The lower dimensional components of your SELF are still aspects of your Multidimensional SELF, but YOU have raised your *primary focus* into the higher dimensions of reality. Please remember, that these expressions are NOT lined up in a third dimensional manner. They are all interwoven and intermingled within the NOW of the ONE.

You will find that as your consciousness expands into the higher frequencies of expression, your third dimensional thinking will become increasingly cumbersome and somewhat obsolete. Hence, you will begin to forget how to think in that old-fashioned manner and unconsciously think from your Multidimensional SELF.

The side effect of this experience might make you think that you are getting dementia or some other earth condition. The truth is that you are expanding beyond ALL 3-D earthly conditions and are discovering that your old way of thinking is exceedingly cumbersome.

Why would you need a buggy whip when you are driving an automobile? Therefore, why would you need a sequential language of separate words when you think within the limitless, timeless NOW? Once your focus is firmly planted in your Planetary Expression of SELF, you will be aligned with Gaia's time.

Gaia is expanding her Focus into Her fifth dimensional SELF. Hence, Her polarities of past and future are collapsing into the NOW, and 3D time is closing. Once you are fully aligned with Gaia's NOW, there will not be time as you know it. You will know time, but not as passing moments in which you must do something or be somewhere. You will begin to adjust your thinking into the limitless, timeless NOW.

Your Super-subconscious animal self, who is very comfortable with the NOW, will begin to fulfill the "ideals" that are passed into it via your Oversoul. An ideal differs from an idea in that an *ideal* is a Divine Concept that your consciousness has been able to embrace. You have been able to embrace these concepts because you have expanded your focus from your deepest, Super-subconscious animal self into your seventh dimensional Oversoul SELF.

Your Super-subconscious holds the codes and patterns of all your earthly incarnations. This component of your being steadily opens once you have focused your attention on the HERE and NOW Beingness of your animal self. Conversely, your Oversoul holds the codes and patterns of all the incarnations you have experienced in your current Galaxy.

Your connection to your Oversoul steadily expands once you have placed your primary *sense of self* into your Galactic SELF. With this expanded perspective of your SELF, you will have completed the Alpha/Omega of your Planetary SELF, and are then totally prepared to release all components of your denser, human form in order to return to your Galactic SELF.

All these processes of ascension overlap so that our ascending ones will always have a solid, familiar format, as well as a perceivable potential locked in to their consciousness. Hence, the ascension process is much like crossing a rushing stream by walking from one stone to the next.

You start on the shore, and then place one foot onto a steppingstone. You do not place your second foot on the next stone until you are certain that it will hold your weight. Then, you will keep your foot on that stone while you test the next stone with your other foot.

All of our ascending ones have expanded their consciousness beyond their Individual/Personal SELF. However, some of them are still attached to their Familial/Cultural SELF, which will keep them from releasing their perceived family, cultural and national obligations and/or attachments.

There is nothing *wrong* with maintaining this attachment, but when you allow your family, culture and nation to hold you back from your process of ascension, you are not able to assist with Planetary Ascension. Not participating in Planetary Ascension greatly limits your process of Personal Ascension, as Gaia is offering a *free* ride into the fifth dimensional expression of reality.

However, those who remain attached to the third/fourth dimensional concepts of family, culture and nations will not be able to adhere their consciousness to the Unity Consciousness of Planetary Ascension. Within Unity Consciousness, every being is of the same ability and power.

In fact, many children, and even infants, are more aligned with ascension than their parents who have had a lifetime of brainwashing. Cultures and Nations divide Gaia's planet and restrict Unity Consciousness to Family, Cultural or national Consciousness. To *catch the wave* of Planetary Ascension you need to blend your consciousness into the immense Flow of Planetary ascension.

A New Home

Those who maintain the 3-D hooks of family, culture and nation (which include the religious and scientific 3-D thinking) will remain in the illusion of third dimensional Earth for as long as that hologram is running. They still have time to expand their consciousness if they choose.

Also, once the final remnants of darkness are expelled from the body of Gaia, the cycles of fear that hold the third dimensional attachments in place will be completed. This fear is closer to being vanquished than you may think, because of you the ascending ones, who have become Masters of your Emotions and expelled fear from your consciousness.

Fear is not alive like love. Love, especially unconditional love, is a living creative force seeking a being through which it can be expressed. Fear, on the other hand, is the "Grim Reaper," who cuts back the old and dying so that the new can be created and nurtured by love. Hence, fear is a necessary component of a third/fourth dimensional reality that is bound to a planetary existence.

When people, families and nations could not leave the planet in search of a new home in the ever-expanding Galaxy, members of the planet believed that they cannot find enough of what they need. This fear became embedded so deeply in the consciousness of many incarnated ones that they killed others to assure that they would *have enough*.

Predation for possession and power over others is the result of the Earthling's Draconian DNA. This

DNA is very strong and powerful, as well as highly intelligent and decisive. However, if the human carries too much fear, they can easily move into the kill-or-be-killed mindset of that DNA. On the other hand, through Mastering your thoughts and emotions, you can use that DNA to assist yourself—rather than to control others.

Becoming the Master of your Energy allows you conscious transit into your seventh dimensional Oversoul, which is the storehouse of ALL your Galactic knowledge, gifts, experiences and incarnations. Just as the Super-subconscious holds the codes and patterns for your Planetary SELF, the Oversoul holds the codes and patterns for your Galactic Self.

It is through activating these codes that you can consciously connect with us, your Galactic Family. When you meet, commune and intertwine with on your Galactic expressions of SELF you will regain your Galactic perception of reality. During your ascension process, many of you will enter into intimate relationships with the YOU who is holding a higher dimensional expression.

Of course, you have many expressions of your Galactic SELF, just as you have many expressions of your human self. When you can fall into the Flow and surrender into the FEEL of your Galactic SELF you can remember how to live two, simultaneous realities. With practice, you will be able to experience more and more simultaneous realities within the NOW of the ONE.

In this manner, you will regain connection with your Galactic Expression of SELF. Your Galactic expressions are aligned with you in the NOW and are offering you a *hand up* into the fifth dimension. Every experience that you can remember having with your Multidimensional SELF is a gift that we ask you to share with the members of your ascending reality.

We will allow you *time* to ponder what we have shared so far, and return shortly so that Mytre can share his first experience of the Seventh Dimensional Oversoul of our Mothership.

The Mothership's Oversoul

MYTRE SPEAKS:

I had not been on the Ship very long when I had my first experience of the Mothership's Oversoul. I had been there long enough to understand that the Ship was a living, multidimensional being. I had a vague understanding of the sixth dimensional areas of the ship. However, the seventh dimensional portion of the Ship is not an "area." It is a formless Soul that overlooks all the Souls who reside on the Ship.

The Super-subconscious frequency of the Ship automatically observes, repairs and updates the basic structure, which is always changing. Therefore it holds the basic form of every component of the Ship. On the other hand, the Oversoul Consciousness is a formless, yet tangible energy that feels like an electrical field filled with love and cohesiveness.

These feelings usually are most predominant on the upper areas of the Ship, such as the Bridge and all command centers. However when necessary, the Oversoul over-lights meetings, individuals, and devices on the Ship that are called upon to function at an exceptionally high state of consciousness.

I was taken to the Mothership shortly after I had left "time" during my meditation. Once I could leave time, a vast array of new abilities where just beyond my reach. Hence, I was taken to the Mothership for more advanced studies. The Arcturian and I entered a Scout Ship and headed for the Mothership. There were just the two of us in the Ship.

I discovered later that the Arcturian could have simply bi-located us to the Mothership, but It wanted us to advance our relations beyond teacher/student into friends. It was then that I began to realize what a wonderful sense of humor that Arcturians have. The Arcturian and I had a chance to chat about whatever came into our minds, and the Arcturian actually made jokes about our experiences together.

I had the chance to see my self through the perception of a higher dimensional Being. This was a bit rough on my ego, which was the point. When I could laugh at my prior fears and misconceptions, I felt many ego-attachments begin to fade from my mind. By the time we arrived at the Mothership, I had released most of my insecurities about being "good enough," as well as my fears of going to the Mothership.

It was not that I was afraid to go to the Mothership. In fact, I was very excited and honored to be able to visit that Ship. However, I started our trip to the Mothership with great apprehension about what I would be called upon to *do*. Fortunately, because of the Arcturians humorous bantering, I was totally relaxed by the time the planetary sized Mothership came into our view.

I must say that my first sight of the Mothership was completely overwhelming. At the same time, it was a mystical experience. I had been training to perceive reality multidimensionally. Hence, I could clearly see the third/fourth dimensional holographic projection, which the Ship sometimes wore, as well as the fifth dimensional over-glow of that hologram, the sixth dimensional light matrix and the seventh dimensional emanation of Pure Spirit and All Knowing.

I also felt the eighth through tenth dimensional energy patterns of the Mothership, as well as patterns of the Arcturians and other Beings of that resonance. I KNEW that there were energy patterns beyond the tenth dimensions, but could not perceive them with any clarity at that time. The Arcturian touched my High Heart, and I received a brief experience of those higher dimensions.

Unfortunately, the resonant frequency of my mental processing was too low to retain any details of that experience. Nonetheless, I stored that FEELING in my High Heart, exactly where the Arcturian touched me. I vowed to believe that soon I would be able to fully experience this cherished moment.

I will skip now to the point at which I had been studying in the Mothership for a while. I cannot give an exact amount of time, as time does not really exist at this level of consciousness. Conversely, those of us who were new to the Inter-

Galactic Training Program were given quarters in which a period of day would be followed by a period of night.

We were to remain in these quarters until we were able to focus our primary consciousness on our fifth dimensional SELF. Our fifth dimensional expression of SELF no longer needed the illusion of the passage of time, the fatigue that that illusion created or the sleep that was necessary to release the illusion of fatigue.

I quickly made friends with my roommates, but found myself constantly missing the Arcturian. One *day* I caught myself being impatient with my roommates. This upset me greatly, as I knew it was a sign that my consciousness was slipping into the lower frequencies rather than expanding into the higher frequency. I excused myself and went to the Nature Area.

There is a huge section of the Mothership that is dedicated to Nature Areas. These areas were holographic, but you absolutely could not tell that when you were there. Once, when I asked the Arcturian why the 3/4D Nature Area was holographic, and it said,

"All reality in the third and fourth dimension are holographic projections from the higher dimensions of reality."

I started to ask my Arcturian friend to explain that concept to me but It disappeared in front of my eyes. Then, where the Arcturian had just been standing/floating, was a huge tree with birds, squirrels and other animals living off of the bio-system of that one tree. I moved forward to touch the tree, but there was a flash of light and the Arcturian stood where there was once a tree.

"Do you see how I projected the hologram of Nature?"

The Arcturians are very good at "one picture is worth a thousand words." At the same time, I realized that my consciousness had become so low in frequency that I had forgotten the basic premises that I had been taught.

"I have to leave the Rookie's Quarters," I blurted out. "My consciousness is dropping because I am entraining with the new-comers, rather than with you or the Ship."

"We are happy that you realize that," the Arcturian said, as it vanished.

OK, I knew the drill now; I had to figure it out for myself. If I wanted to move beyond my present quarters I would have to prove—to myself—that I was ready. I had become so overcome by the mere vision of the Mothership that I had allowed my consciousness to drop back down to a familiar resonance.

I discovered that the Rookie Quarters, as we had named them, were no longer comfortable because I had grown beyond it. I had needed more of the illusion of time to figure that out. Since I was on my own, I had to figure out how to convince myself that I WAS ready to release all the familiar markers of reality and fully embrace my new life.

Since *leaving time* had gotten me to the Mothership, and being placed in a time-bound area for new students was so frustrating, the solution was for me to release time again. However, I had to remember how I had released time in the first place.

What I had unconsciously done, I now had to do consciously and intentionally. What if I went back in time to when I first saw the Mothership from the Scout Ship? What if I could go back in time and perceive the Mothership with love and acceptance rather than the fear of being overwhelmed?

That sounded like a good idea, but I had no idea how to do it. Then, I thought of the glowing energy around the Mothership that the Arcturian had called the Oversoul. The Arcturian had said that the Oversoul holds the codes and patterns of all the Soul Records of everyone who was living or visiting the Ship. These Soul Records contain all the multidimensional experiences that each Soul had ever experienced.

Within my present body, I was clearly Pleiadian. However, I had suspected for quite a while that there was a large element of Arcturian Nature within my Being. I even had a dim memory of being Arcturian, but I could not recover any details of that expression of my Multidimensional SELF.

Yes, my Multidimensional SELF could pull my resonance into the higher expressions of my being; that is if I could trust my experience. I had just experienced how easily I could lose trust in myself, and I was not going to do so again. I would ask my Multidimensional SELF how to leave time, as I had done before, by reading my Soul Records in the Oversoul of the Mothership.

I was alone in the Holosuite, so I sat down to mediate and quickly moved into a deep trance. The first thing that I realized was that I had prepared all my life, in fact for many of my lives, for this opportunity to assist with the ascension of our chosen planet in the Pleiades. With that realization I began to consciously *feel* all that I would need to release in order to move into the expression of my SELF that could fulfill the task of conscious ascension.

The Arcturians had seen this ability, but I still could not. I had remembered and visited many of my multidimensional realities while studying with the Arcturian on the other Starship. Then the Arcturian had chosen me for this special training, but all I could feel was what I would have to release. In order to continue my training I would have to release my ties to my old world and move into the unknown.

With this realization, myriad doubts were uncovered from their hiding places. How could I assist my planet to go into the unknown of the fifth dimension when I could not even go into the unknown of my own mind? I would have to confront the part of myself that was afraid to move into the unknown and was quietly holding me back. I had learned to control my life.

However, would I be able to continually surrender to the higher worlds as the Arcturian was teaching me? Or would I tenaciously hold onto what remained of the life I had previously lived? There it was, the life I HAD lived. What life had I lived that needed my attention before I could go forward and release the need for TIME, once and for all?

With that question, I felt the Pure Spirit and All Knowing of the Mothership's Oversoul wrap around me like a warm cloud. Within this safety and comfort I could release my hidden fears of what I would have to release, what I would have to do and who I would have to become in order to be *good enough* to fulfill the honored task for which the Arcturians had chosen me.

With the Oversoul around me, I could hear my higher expressions of SELF cheering me on, but I could not move forward yet. I had to release the burden of my hidden insecurities, fears and confusions. I could feel that I was leaving *time,* so I could not release them later, nor could I release them in my future. There was only NOW. Therefore, I allowed them to come to the surface of my awareness so that I could love them free, once and for all.

I found that my heaviest burden was the need to do it right, the need to be *good enough* in the eyes of others. But who were these others? Where were they now? Why was I still carrying them in my consciousness? In response to these questions the Oversoul embraced me more tightly and *time* was gone. I could feel the difference in my thinking, my emotions and within whatever connection I still had to my body.

Free of *time*, I began to float through memory bands of myriad incarnations. Brief pictures and emotions floated through my mind as I passed by each reality, as my journey continued. I knew that the Oversoul was taking me to a certain reality, the reality that still held a sense of failure. I could feel that sense of failure growing stronger, but I was strangely detached from it.

I was out of *time*, so I had no idea how long I traveled through the files of the Oversoul, but as I continued I became calmer and more detached from the passing realties. Then suddenly, a reality moved towards me like a beaming Sun. I could not float past it, even though I wanted to. There was unfinished business in that life that I had to complete in order to free my consciousness from some invisible burden.

Suddenly the "Sun" was before me and pulled me in with such force that I almost passed out. However, I reminded myself that *I AM the Master of my MIND.* This sentence opened a portal into a planet in chaos and I heard, "The Ascension of Arcturus."

Join us in Book Two to continue with the Pleiadian Perspective on Ascension.

A Glimpse of Book Two of Pleiadian Perspectives on Ascension

As the file of the Oversoul opened, it pulled me in to a scene from before all counting of time. At first, I could only hear words I did not understand and feel a sense of panic. Eventually, I regained my vision enough to see a scene before me that struck my heart as it reminded me of my Homeworld in the Pleiades.

Beings, who looked vaguely humanoid, were rushing around in a near state of panic. Something was happening to their planet that they could not understand. My first thought was, "How could these frightened beings be Arcturians?" An instant response, seemingly from the Oversoul was, "They are not still Arcturians. There are some among them who will remember to return to being Arcturian."

The Oversoul then told me how formless Beings had come from a distant universe to visit the young Milky Way Galaxy. These Beings had never known form, nor had they every lived on a planet. The name of these Beings is impossible to translate into any sequential language, such as the one I am using to share my story. Therefore, I will call them "Pre-Arcturians".

These Pre-Arcturians decided to have the experience of "Being a Planet," since being an individual was far below their conception. For millions of cycles they attached their great consciousness to the orb and the atmosphere of a planet. Eventually, they desired the experience of having forms that could move around the planet.

They decided that in this manner they could have the different perspective of being ON the planet, rather than BEING the planet. For countless cycles of the planet, some of them lived within their somewhat humanoid forms. On the other hand, the Oneness held the form of the planet and its atmosphere, so that it could be protected and maintained.

Eventually, the planet lowered in frequency enough to have a vague relationship with time. With the new development of time, which was a unique experience for the Arcturians, things began to happen that were not initiated by the Arcturians who where the planetary holders of form...

About the Author:

Suzanne Lie PhD began her website, www.multidimensions.com under the penname of Suzan Caroll in 1996. Since then she added the website of www.suzanneliephd.com and www.creatingnewearth.com.

Suzanne has also written the novels:

Thirty Veils of Illusion
Visions from Venus Trilogy
Visions from Venus
Reconstructing Reality
Remembering the Return

Becoming One ~ A Manual for Personal and Planetary Ascension Volumes I and II

Seven Steps to Soul ~ A Poetic Journey of Spiritual Awakening

What Did You Learn? ~ An Illustrated Story About Creating Planetary Ascension

The Short Stories

The Violet Temple
A Child's Adventure in Faerie ~ For The Child Within Us All

Additional Information about the Author

Who exactly is the author of the book? Is the author Suzanne Lie who typed the words? Is the author Mytre, Mytria or even the Arcturian who sent the words into her consciousness?

If she only knew what would happen after she had written it, does that make her the author? Or, does that make her the scribe?

Perhaps the question is, which persona of Suzanne is the author? Is she an extension of Mytre, Mytria and/or the Arcturian? Or, is she none of the characters and they are only in her imagination?

Furthermore, is the information in this book true, or is it pure fantasy? How often is science fiction future fact?

What do you, the reader, chose as your fact? Can you believe that this story is true? Or, do you prefer to believe that this story is pure fiction?

If you cannot answer these questions yet, perhaps you will discover them as you read the Books Two, Three, and maybe even Book Four.

Please return for the next books about the, ***Pleiadian Perspective on Ascension.***

Suzanne Lie PhD

Suzanne Lie earned her PhD in Clinical Psychology in 1984 and has been a practicing as an MFT psychotherapist since 1986. She lives in the South Bay of Southern California beside the beautiful Pacific Ocean. Suzanne is married with two children and 4 grandchildren.

If you wish to contact Dr. Lie you can email her at:
suzancaroll@multidimensions.com

Suzanne Lie

For more info visit

http://www.multidimensions.com/TheVision/books.html

Awakening With Suzanne Lie ~ an ongoing blog since September of 2009

http://suzanneliephd.blogspot.com

Multidimensional Meditations ~ YouTube site since 2010

http://www.youtube.com/user/suzannelie

A New Home

Reviews are greatly appreciated. Thank you.

Made in the USA
Lexington, KY
14 February 2015